TARTTS 5

Incisive Fiction
from
Emerging Writers

Joe Taylor, editor

Tricia Taylor, editor

Livingston Press
The University of West Alabama

The rights to all these stories reside with the individual authors. Some of the stories
have appeared previously in the following magazines
"See the Mississippi" by Dan Pope, in *Night Train 2*
"Catapult" by Emily Fridlund, in *Chariton Review*
"House of Guns"by Mary Helen Specht, in *Florida Review*
"Gutted" by Gregg Cusick, excerpted in *Saturday Evening Post*

Table of Contents

*Winner

~Tourmaline~

CB Anderson

Six days out of seven John polished stones in back while Evie sat out front to set them. Although the shop was small they talked only at noon, when Evie turned down the radio and they ate lunch at John's workbench. The meals were spare, the conversation sparer. Afterward she would resume her position by the window, squinting at the stones arrayed in front of her. On fair days, during the hours the sun traced an arc from the Methodist church to the courthouse, the stones shone, but dully because Evie and John didn't carry quality gems. You could hardly call them gems; they were rocks, really—milk and smoky quartz, some herderite and mica fashioned into the earrings and necklaces that sold just well enough to allow Evie and John to keep up their house on the edge of town. Their customers were young people who lived back from the bay and possessed neither the means nor the longings that led the moneyed crowd to shop downcoast in Portland.

Tuesdays the shop was closed. On those days John and Evie got up early and drove two hours inland into western Maine, to the abandoned mines they'd been picking for thirty years. Every few months they rotated sites. That November it was Glassface, on the far side of Newry. Evie waited for these mornings, the coffee-steamed windows inside the truck, the pewter horizon that brightened as they drove. The weight between her and John was lighter then, eased by the dislocation of time and place. She liked the walk past slag piles to the base of the hill, then the hike up and over the pegmatic top to outcroppings on the face. The thousand small decisions of where to place her feet emptied her mind of everything else.

Each time they went a little deeper to locate fresh rock, and all of it—the feel of ledge beneath her boots, the cold air, even the paltriness of the take—was somehow reassuring until the afternoon

Evie discovered a vein of tourmaline in a pocket beyond where they'd ever dug before. She found it by chance, having gone off by herself to escape the wind and sit for a minute. The mouth looked like any other, granite-rimmed and dusky with junk rock, but then she spotted a faint green shine on the left wall of the crevice. When she tapped with her pick, it felt as if the surface were striking back. "I might have something," she called.

John was beside her in seconds. He shucked off his pack, wedged himself into the pocket. "Hand me my lamp."

Evie rummaged in his pack with the thought that the shine would turn out to be pyrite or mica. She was wrong. Within a half hour John had chiseled loose two half-inch rods of tourmaline, which, when he held them out to her, caught the sun so sharply her eyes watered. "They're pretty."

"Pretty? They're goddamn beautiful," John said. One hand cupped the crystals, the other was clenched at his side. A bloody scratch extended from his nose to ear.

By dusk they'd freed seven crystals: three green, two pink, two watermelon. Before they left John covered the crevice with brush weighted with boulders. Evie helped, though she thought the branches only drew attention. No one had found the vein in hundreds of years; it was a fluke she'd seen it today.

At seven, when they were finally off the rock, the light in the woods intensified to ochre then disappeared. A few last leaves rattled overhead, dry and brittle as bird bones, and cold closed in around them. John was whistling, the tourmaline tightly wrapped in the bandana he usually wore on his head. Strands of hair across his balding crown blew free. Evie couldn't recall the last time she'd heard him whistle, tried to feel his happiness and came up blank. Her temples ached. She was hungry, tired, pleased by the find but wary of the suddenness with which fortune had presented itself.

Nor was she all that fond of tourmaline. It seemed to her a showy gem, loud and indelicate. Still, the next day—having been restored by lentil soup and early bed—when she sat down to a watermelon crystal John had gotten up at five to cut, she found it more agreeable than she'd expected. The green and pink merged well, and it invited touch. After some deliberation she decided on a bracket setting. In platinum—usually she worked in sterling or gold plate, but this called for something finer. She would hang the stone in a beveled frame and handmake a chain, broadening the links as they neared the center.

All morning while Evie tapped and soldered, people stopped outside the window to watch. Beneath their gaze she felt transformed. It was as easy to make a beautiful piece of jewelry as a mediocre one if you had the right materials. Several bystanders—a woman with twins in a stroller, a handsome older couple—stepped into the shop for a closer look. From beside her the tourmaline winked in its velvet bed. "What a lovely stone," said the older man. "Where did it come from?"

Evie hesitated. "I, we—"

John appeared from the back. "Can I help?"

"I was wondering about the tourmaline."

"We buy it from a wholesaler." The lie surprised Evie, but John's hand held steady on her shoulder.

The man took in a case of inexpensive hoops hung with bits of quartz, then looked again at the tourmaline. "I didn't know you carried things like this."

"We do."

After the couple left, John's hand stayed on her back, and Evie thought of resting her head against his belly. He ran his finger down one of her braids. "We may make some money yet."

John wanted things she didn't care about: a bigger house, a boat and—more intangibly—a certitude of stance he'd equated with affluence throughout their 35-year marriage. Evie was forming a response, a cautious one that would acknowledge his statement without endorsing it, when the phone rang.

"Just leave it," John said.

But when the machine clicked on, the line went dead. The caller ID gave the number as restricted. Evie's palms began to itch. "It's Phip. I know it is."

John shrugged, turned to go. "That man who just left is exactly the kind of customer we want," he said. As the sun swung out from behind the church, the walls brightened and shafts of light striped the floor.

~

Years earlier Evie had thought John's coolness toward their son stemmed from the fact that they'd been nearing forty when he was born. John hadn't wanted any children and Evie, relieved to be away from a too-large family ruled by laxity and noise, had gone along. Then Phip arrived—a colicky baby who grew into a high-strung boy—and even as Evie filled with fierce and unanticipated love she sensed John's distance, maybe his embarrassment. It was easier for her than for him to connect with a child who disliked sports and preferred his own company to that of other kids. "Too much air and not enough earth," John said, as if Phip were alchemy gone wrong. Only later, when Phip turned into a teenager who excelled in school but couldn't wield a saw or miter a joint, did Evie begin to understand that the rift between them originated in likeness rather than in difference.

Phip himself did much to explain it one Saturday in the shop, during the spring of his senior year. That morning John had shown him how to operate the tumbler with the expectation that after lunch Phip would polish the quartz John cut. But then, after the three of them sat peaceably enough at the workbench eating sandwiches, Phip cracked the tumbler by overloading it. John began to curse, and Phip let the last few rocks drop to the floor. *I'm just like you,* he shouted, and Evie's heart caught. They looked so similar—the fine sandy hair and too-thin skin that splotched when excited or upset. In a rush she recalled the week John had spent trying to repair the tumbler last month when he jammed it, his frustration at finally having to send it out instead. She jumped up, knocking aside the workbench in her haste—"Stop!"—but by then John had shoved Phip away from the tumbler and Phip was crying.

Several weeks later Phip graduated and left to hitchhike to the northwest, ostensibly for the summer. That was eighteen months ago. The last time Evie had heard from him was October. He was in Seattle, working the counter at a Sears automotive shop and rooming with a couple of university students. Before Seattle he'd been in Eugene. His calls home were infrequent and unapologetic. Evie was, she understood, guilty by association and probably more. Recently the shop phone had started ringing around noontime once or twice a week. Each time the

CB Anderson

caller hung up after Evie said hello. She felt sure it was Phip, unwilling to talk yet wanting them to know he was alright, although John scoffed when she told him. "He's out there hanging around without a care," he said. But Evie imagined Phip steadier now, matured, wishing he hadn't left the way he did.

~

In the month that followed Evie's find on Glassface, John himself seemed steadier—less inclined to outbursts and able to sleep without tossing. Business was picking up. They'd sold three tourmaline necklaces and a couple of rings, which tripled their normal income, and the safe in the rear of the store held several dozen crystals. Evie was staying in Castine to work and tend the shop while John, returned to an ambitious younger self, drove daily to the vein. At night he'd taken to reading jewelers' catalogs, overproduced glossies from New York and Los Angeles that disoriented Evie but seemed to please him. When she spooned him from behind to sleep, he let her stay instead of complaining that she made him overheat. In those moments Evie felt almost grateful to the tourmaline, to the renewed prospect of success—if such a thing might bring them closer.

She glanced at him in the thinning dark of the truck cab. It was a Tuesday—this week she'd insisted on coming too. John looked tanned and ruddy, as if it were July rather than late December. The cut on his cheek had healed to be replaced by others. Evie lifted the lid from her coffee, inhaled. Nascent light washed through the cab; the sun was coming up. Always it rose faster than it set. "Feels great to be out," she said, which it did. Getting dressed she'd imagined a moment like this one, and another on the trail as her hands and feet began to pulse with blood.

John grunted. He hadn't wanted her here, argued that it made more sense for her to stay in the shop. If he'd known how close she'd come to selling another necklace yesterday—a man shopping for a thirtieth anniversary gift for his wife had promised to return this morning—he would have argued harder. But Evie was glad to be going to the mine. Today, at least, things wouldn't be just on his terms.

Near Standish a deer dashed across the road. Evie braced for more, but John barely seemed to notice. The tips of his fingers were red and abraded: rock burn. "I contacted a dealer," he said.

"What?"

"Got his name from the back of Aufiero."

It took Evie a moment to realize he was referring to one of the catalogs he studied in the evenings. She wedged her coffee lidless into its holder. "What do you mean?"

"He handles tourmaline." John looked over at her. "Could you cover that?"

Evie dropped the lid onto her cup. Outside was a blur of bare trees and houses of the large but run-down sort that reminded her of theirs.

"You know the piece you just finished?" John asked. "That's good enough to sell anywhere. Even better than the ones I showed him."

"You showed someone my work?"

"Last Wednesday in Portland, after I drove out to the mine. He was up from Boston."

Evie thought back to dinnertime last week. The only image she came up with was herself pulling into the Burger Barn for take-out, eating fries from the bag on her way home. "You should've told me."

"I forgot." John grinned, his crow's feet intersecting the lines around his mouth.

"You should've told me."

"Jesus, Mary and Joseph. Can't you just be happy?" John pressed the accelerator then let up again. Evie hated his stop-and-go driving, his under and overreactions. She bit down hard on her lip, determined to preserve the outing.

They drove through Newry Center. The town green was quiet, sheep and goats from the live crèche still bedded down in hay. Evie tried to imagine the meeting between John and the dealer from Boston. What had he worn? Had he carried her pieces in his pocket, and why hadn't she noticed them missing?

~

On the top of Glassface it was beginning to snow. Evie struggled for footing as she and John traversed the slippery granite. The site, when they reached it, looked innocuous enough concealed, but as John pulled away the brush she could see he'd widened the mouth

CB Anderson

considerably. Uncovered, it gaped up at them and Evie shivered.

"It's deeper than you'd think," John said with satisfaction. Evie was taken by the sudden vision of a gem-lined cave, so out of place in the hills of western Maine. She didn't want to enter, but already John had unpacked their lamps and fitted his onto his forehead. "Watch for shards," he said, crawling in ahead of her. Evie's knees ached as she followed.

Inside John busied himself on the far wall. He'd done a lot of work here too, exposed several lines of schorl that seeped water when she touched. Rocks were piled near the opening, and junk stone littered the floor. It was cramped enough that to sit Evie had to fold her knees to her chest. She closed her eyes while overhead John chiseled.

"Hell yes," she heard him say. When she opened her eyes he was near the ceiling on a sill of ledge. Only his feet and legs were visible; the rest of him had disappeared into a chimney. "I need more light," he said, voice muffled by a hundred tons of pegmatite. "Can you shine up here?"

Evie complied then closed her eyes again, disconnected from the cave and from John's single-mindedness. Maybe she did belong in the shop. For the most part she was content working the tourmaline, had grown beguiled by it. Each crystal asked for its own setting, and she was learning to listen. Understanding this was allowing her, when the phone rang at noon, to pick it up and convey the kind of silence that let the caller know she was simply present rather than willing him to speak.

Bits of granite rained down from the ledge. Evie braced for John to fall. If both of them were injured, who would go for help? But when she opened her eyes he was balanced on the sill, now reduced to half a foothold. As he inched right, more rock flaked off. "It's giving way," she said, pressing closer to the wall. "For God's sake, John, watch out!" Already he was stepping sideways into nothing. Evie heard a tearing sound as he slid down hard against the ledge.

Then he was beside her on the floor, forehead and hands raked bloody, holes torn in his ski pants. "I almost had it," he said. "I couldn't quite reach." The abrasions didn't seem to register. He craned his neck, stared up at the place in the ceiling where his claw still hung. It occurred to Evie that he'd probably come at least this close to hurting himself when she wasn't here.

"How much do we really need?" she asked.

"Need?" John's breath blew hot on her neck. "That's not the point. It's here, and it's ours." He gestured to the left side of the wall, where the rock was least worn and small lips protruded from the surface. For the first time all day he looked at her directly. "It won't hold me, but it will you."

Evie's chest broke out in sweat. "What if it gives way?"

"You'll be fine."

Long ago, on one of their first dates, they'd built a birdhouse—hours of silent concentration—and as they cut and glued Evie had given herself over to John's quiet ways. It was several years into their marriage before she learned his reserve concealed a white-hot core capable of lasting sullenness or wrath.

The white mouth of the cave seemed a long way off. More than anything Evie wanted to be back outside, with the wind and snow around her. Instead she stood, used the lips to climb and, when she was wedged high enough, took John's claw to unpack what he'd started: an inch-long rod of watermelon shining in the half-light.

~

The next morning when she arrived at the shop, the man who'd been in for an anniversary gift was waiting on the sidewalk. "Here you are." He thumped a rolled-up newspaper against his thigh. "I came yesterday too."

The white hair and tweed coat—suddenly Evie recognized him not just as Monday's customer but as the man who'd watched while she worked her first piece of tourmaline a month earlier. A regular: the thought cheered her. In spite of yesterday's near-fall, John had gone to Newry again this morning, driving off before Evie even realized he was out of bed. She rose at 5:30 and waited three hours to leave the house.

Inside, the man watched as she unlocked the safe. "How long have you been working tourmaline?"

"Not too long. But we've been making other jewelry here for years."

"Well, I admire quality work." He pointed to a necklace from the tray of finished pieces. "May I?"

She placed the pendant on the show board. "I like the way the color changes with the angle. That's why I free-set it, to show the shades of pink."

"My wife will love it." He stood by the counter while she wrapped. "Do you and your husband play bridge?"

Evie hesitated. "Not very well."

"Golf? Our group plays until it snows."

Evie shook her head. She'd never held a club.

"Perhaps dinner sometime then."

After he left, Evie wondered about the overture of friendship. Had the tourmaline transformed her and John into worthwhile social prospects? They'd spent decades in Castine with few friends other than their next-door neighbors, who raised goats in a boggy field, and the owners of Dunn's fish shop on the wharf. Phip hadn't been the sort of child whose hobbies linked them to other families, nor had anyone else seemed all that interested. It would please John that someone had asked them out to dinner. She'd mention it when he got back.

She tuned the radio to the BBC news, then, still restless, to classical music from Mount Washington. It played sporadically, with an overlay of static. After a few minutes she switched it off. In the silence she began to sing—softly, lest the florist next door hear—and gave herself to the work of finishing a pair of earrings. The phone rang when she was halfway through *The Bramble and the Rose*. 'Restricted,' the caller ID said. She glanced at her watch: already 11:30.

By the time Evie got to it, the phone had rung three times and she'd decided to speak. "We love you," she said into the receiver. "Just come on home."

There was silence on the other end. "Phip?" she said. "Are you okay out there?"

"This is Norman Packer. May I please speak to John?"

Chagrin made Evie bold. "You must be the dealer. The one my husband met last week."

"That's right." The man cleared his throat. "Your work is beautiful. I can help you sell it."

She gripped the receiver. "Thanks, but we're doing alright on our own."

After Evie hung up, lunchtime shoppers filtered in. She barely greeted them, didn't feel like talking or eating lunch herself. Nor did she feel like working anymore. As the sun slid out from behind the church, the tourmaline glowed but she ignored it. A girl in a sweatshirt rummaged the quartz hoops, asked if there were more. "What we have is there," Evie said, and the girl recoiled at her tone.

It was true—the racks were depleted, the jewelry tarnished. She and John had spent so much time on tourmaline the other stock had gone ignored. Evie started to polish and rearrange, then decided she didn't care. Instead she sat behind the register and stared through the window at the sun, which reached a low zenith before dropping toward the courthouse. She began to nurse a dark thought: Phip was in trouble and afraid to tell them. Maybe he didn't have the means to make it home.

She was still sitting when the door jangled and John came in. Sunspots in her field of vision stippled his face. "You certainly left early this morning," she said.

He pulled off his bandana. "Had an idea about how to access that top-tier stuff. A little bit of blasting."

"Blasting? Are you serious? The whole thing will collapse."

"It's the only way of getting at what's left."

"We've taken enough."

"No. After all these years, we've earned more." In his expression Evie read the impossibility of backing down. "Did anyone call?"

Evie fiddled with the *void* key. "No."

"We're supposed to drive to Boston on Friday to see that dealer. Bring all our new stuff. He said he'd leave directions."

"We can manage our own work." The cash drawer popped open. "Anyway, I sold another piece today. We're doing so well."

"We need to ratchet things up. Finish as much work as you can."

"I don't want to go to Boston, John."

"Then I'll go alone."

She stood up. "Sure you will." Whenever they went south she was the one who took the wheel. John drove inland to the mines, but he couldn't handle congestion, cars too close or too fast.

"I'll take the damn bus."

She went home by herself. When John hadn't shown up for two hours she put on canned soup and ate in front of the TV. The idea of dinner out with the customer and his wife seemed foolish now; they had nothing in common at all.

Around her the old pipes whistled and banged, the noise disproportionate to the meager heat delivered. Evie decided to light the stove, pulled on boots to gather wood from the porch but John had cut only trunk rounds and there wasn't any kindling. Back inside she searched for newspaper and found the lot of it had gone out with the trash. Then, on the bedside table, she spotted John's foot-high stack of catalogs. They slipped and slid as she gathered them in her arms.

Kneeling in front of the stove, she tore the first catalog's cover—a Mikimoto pearl ensemble—crumpled it and threw it in. The pages resisted being balled, so smooth and heavy was the paper, but Evie kept at it. When she'd packed the stove she lit a match. The pile popped, sucked and then ignited. She tore off more pages and fed those in sections at a time, finally whole catalogs at once. The room stank of chemicals—ink, chlorine, lacquer—and her head ached. But the fire was throwing off jets of turquoise laced with purple, so she let it burn.

~

In the morning John's side of the bed was still smooth, and Evie felt hung over. Already it was after nine. Downstairs she peered into the refrigerator—eggs, pancakes, all of it seemed like too much trouble. Instead she settled for half a cantaloupe and went back upstairs to bed to eat. As wind pushed at the windows she chewed halfheartedly and wondered why they'd never bothered to insulate the house.

By the time she drove down to the shop it was nearly 10:30. John's truck was parked outside. Evie's heart pumped with irritation and relief as she pulled in behind him and got out. Inside, he was sitting at her desk by the window, a tray of unset tourmaline in front of him.

"You're late," he said as she came in.

"Where were you last night?"

"Here."

The shop had no couch, no easy chair, not even a rug. "Doing what?"

"This." He tapped the tray. "I told you, we need to finish everything by Friday."

"How come you're not in Newry with your dynamite?"

"Right now this matters more."

Evie leaned closer. His joints were over-soldered, the bevel too shallow to grip properly. It was a waste of effort. John himself looked steeped in fatigue—shoulders slack, cheeks drawn tight against the bone. Remnants of take-out Chinese lay on the desk.

"You should go home and sleep."

His jaw jerked. "Don't tell me what to do."

Evie sighed. The whole shop felt unfamiliar—the radio was tuned to a talk show, jabber over topics no one would remember in a week—and it smelled of soy sauce and sweat. She thought of a walk, out along the jetty at the end of Main. "I'll be back."

"How are we supposed to make money if you're never here?"

Quickly Evie calculated: Fifty weeks times thirty years yielded something on the order of sixty thousand hours. She zipped her coat.

Bent over his ruined work, John cleared his throat. "By the way, your son's across the street."

Evie could not absorb the words.

"At Cardullo's, having himself a leisurely breakfast."

The shop door banged closed behind her. Inside Cardullo's she spotted Phip in a booth on the far wall. He stood up when she reached him. "You're home," Evie said. "You didn't call, not yesterday at least. I thought—" She choked back a laugh and then a sob.

"I was driving."

"Driving?"

"I bought a truck while I was there."

He gestured outside at a used pick-up. "Blue," Evie pointlessly observed. She reached to hold him, and he didn't pull away.

"It's almost Christmas," he said. He'd grown taller and filled out. His too-short pants were ones she'd bought years earlier, and his hair curled against his nape. Wordlessly she sat. Relief began to settle in around her like a quilt.

Phip pushed his ham and eggs into the middle of the table. Suddenly hungry, Evie picked up a fork. "You've really been okay?" *Tell me everything*, she wanted to say, but held it back. There'd be time for that.

"I'm fine. A little tired." His smile—quick and wide, with slightly lengthened canines—he'd gotten it from her. "I stopped to see you at the shop."

"I slept in." The salt in the ham was puckering her mouth. She stopped chewing. "I burned Dad's catalogs last night."

"Catalogs? Where was he?"

"The shop. Doing my job." She shook her head, backed up. "We found a vein of tourmaline."

"He told me. Said he couldn't take me out to see it because the site had to be secure." Phip laughed, stood up. "I have to use the bathroom."

He'll need new pants, Evie thought as Phip loped away. Some boots, a hair-cut, anything at all. She rummaged in her purse for pen and paper, pulled out a pad with a half-finished drawing. Last night when she'd burned the catalogs she'd come across an article on design. *Each piece reveals its intentions*, it said, which seemed to Evie true. The article discussed things she'd not yet considered—concept, for instance—and brought to mind a piece that had eluded her. In the shop, when John had shown her a rod of watermelon cross-cut into discs, she'd seen only pink interiors rimmed with green. But freed from the constraint of color, she thought of tree rings, each a year's growth. While the fire fumed she began to sketch small leaves to link the first disc to the second, the second to the third.

Now, as waitresses called in their orders, she added a couple more curled leaves. Phip returned and looked over her shoulder. "What's that?"

"A bracelet, I think."

He cracked his knuckles. "Dad'll be happy."

Evie's eyes filled. "Phip. I shouldn't have let you leave like that. It wasn't right. But Dad—"

"It's okay," he said. "Will you make it out of gold?"

Evie sat back. "I don't know." Her thoughts were elsewhere again, on how to mark her son's return.

~

The shrimp looked plump and opalescent, but Dunns' special was haddock at $4.99, so Evie bought three pounds to make a chowder. "Phip's come home," she'd announced to Teresa Dunn when she first walked in, having left him at the house with bags of new clothes and toiletries. Now, as the other woman wrapped the fish and said how glad she was, Evie spontaneously invited her to dinner. "Allen too," she said. "Phip likes you guys, and it's been ages since you were over."

"It has," Teresa agreed. The two couples got together rarely, and when they did it was always at the Dunns' big apartment on top of the fish shop. Even with their six children grown and gone, the place still had a relaxed, robust feel that Evie never had achieved in her own home. A roof deck overlooked the harbor, and ivy wound around the railings. Phip had liked it there; when he turned a year old and John insisted it was time for Evie to go back to work they paid Teresa to baby-sit. Phip didn't mix much with the other kids but he warmed to Teresa. Evie was relieved by that, although she cried for months when she dropped him off. Even now her throat seized at the memory.

She slipped the fish into her tote. "I'm not sure John's so pleased that Phip's home."

"Pffft." Teresa waved her hand. "Nothing's ever easy with him."

It had been weeks since they'd seen each other, and Teresa knew nothing about the tourmaline. Evie started to explain then stopped. What would she tell—the find itself? John's near-fall? The dealer from Boston? Besides, Teresa was smart and caring, but Evie sometimes felt exposed by her pointed observations. "John's been working hard," was all she said. That much, at least, was true.

By seven the kitchen windows were fogged with the simmering chowder. John was reading the paper, and Evie could hear *The Wall* playing upstairs in Phip's room. In spite of the seeming accord, her worry skipped from place to place: dinner would be awkward; Phip would want to stay upstairs; John would discover the remains of his catalogs in the stove.

When the doorbell rang, she rushed from the kitchen. Teresa handed over a plate of brownies, while beside her Allen held a tub

CB Anderson

of ice cream to his chest. "A la mode," he said. Most of Castine's residents, exposed to a lifetime by the sea, grew briny and wrinkled with age but Allen looked less lined, smoother each time Evie saw him. As Phip appeared in the hallway and Allen reached to shake hands, he radiated goodwill.

The ease continued during dinner. Evie put the tureen of chowder in the middle of the table while John uncorked wine. "To good fortune," he said, and if Phip was slighted by the lack of reference to his return it didn't show.

"Yes," said Teresa, "To friendship and to family." They drank, and Evie—flanked on one side by Phip and the other by Teresa—felt buoyed with optimism.

As they ate, Phip described his trip home, how he'd chosen a route through the Rockies then south along the Missouri River. "This country's huge," he said. "You realize the scale when you drive all day through just one state." To Evie he did seem more mature, fuller, as if he'd settled into himself while he was away. It was hard to picture him bolting from the shop, the way he had the day the tumbler broke, or slamming his door on her, as he had when she went upstairs to talk with him later.

"How long were you on the road?" Allen asked.

"Two weeks. But I made a lot of side trips."

The chowder was delicious—rich with potatoes and haddock, and tangy with the parmesan Evie had added on a whim. During seconds, after they'd caught up on the Dunns' eight grandchildren, John began to talk about the tourmaline. The story came more easily than Evie would have thought. Keeping it to herself had made it seem so convoluted.

"We'll have at least fifty carats when we're done."

Allen helped himself to another roll. "How much would you say it's worth?"

John's features hooded over. "I don't know."

"Thirty or forty thousand," Evie said. "The stone, that is. A lot depends on what we do with it."

She felt John's stare before she looked up. It held something—warning or rebuke—and she turned away from it.

"That reminds me, Evie. Packer called again. Why'd you tell him not to?"

"Who's Packer?" asked Phip.

"A dealer," Evie said. Her stomach began to tighten around the chowder. "Your father thinks he'll make us rich."

"A lot more than we've seemed able to manage on our own," John said.

Allen turned to Phip. "How'd your truck hold up?"

Phip was tearing his napkin into strips. "Fine."

John leaned forward. "What I want to know is, what's he going to do now that he's here?"

"Maybe he'll drive you to Boston on Friday." Evie put out her hand to steady Phip's. "What do you think of his new truck?"

"Won't have it long. He'll never keep up the payments."

"I paid cash." Paper fluttered to the floor as Phip stood up.

John reached for the wine. "So what's your plan, anyway?"

Before John had finished filling his glass, Phip was out of the room and at the door. Evie went after him and Teresa followed her. "Go," Teresa said, but already Evie had grabbed her purse and headed down the steps.

~

Phip's pickup smelled of cigarettes and wet socks. He backed out the driveway, shifted through neutral into first and pulled onto the road. "It's so flat here," he said. "In Washington the mountains start closer to the coast." Evie thought of the hills on the other side of Auburn, how they gathered and built until by Newry they had substance.

Her surprise at being in the truck was giving way to something else—acknowledgment if not complete acceptance. "We don't have anything with us," she said.

"I know." Phip turned onto the by-pass that led to the highway.

"Wait. Can you take me to the shop?"

Other than strings of Christmas bulbs, the downtown streets were dark. Inside the shuttered store Evie stood a while without switching on the lights. She knew the place by feel anyway, each dip in the floor, every jutting surface.

In the back room she spun the dial to the safe. It opened with a thud, and she pulled out the tray that held her work. She zipped rings and pendants into her purse along with the watermelon discs, then reached for the case of uncut crystals. It occurred to her to take it all, to leave the shop open with a sign that said *Please Help Yourself*, so that when John showed up the place would be emptied, the cases and racks stripped clean.

"Mom?" Phip stood in the doorway.

Evie swept half the tourmaline into her coat pocket, put back the rest and closed the safe.

"He's such an asshole," Phip said.

The crystals she'd pocketed felt sharp when Evie pressed them with her fingertips. From before: John standing bent with his arms around her, his grassy scent as he fumbled to help her place bits of wood on the birdhouse. They were twenty-two years old.

"He can be," Evie said. She moved slowly toward the front room, toed around the Chinese cartons piled by the trash. It was as if mortar had been loosened from her joints—she might fall; she might move freely.

At her desk the tools were jumbled, her loupe lens-down on the vise. She capped the loupe, piled all of it into a cardboard box Phip handed her.

He opened the door and the cold came in. Reaching into her pocket, Evie pressed hard against another crystal until pinpricks radiated up her arm. They would drive through the night and, after they'd slept, eat breakfast at a truck stop. Later, as Phip took the wheel again and the landscape began to open up, he would tell more about his time away from home. Afterward she would describe the Glassface mine for him—the gem glow, the fall, the Tuesdays that had altogether ceased. By the time the food settled, the tourmaline discs would be laid out across her lap, showing what should happen next.

~Bittersweet~

Charles M. Boyer

Some years ago I had a chance to spend June in Paris. The trip evolved out of several vague conversations with a publisher concerning a book he'd envisioned based on Robert Doisneau's classic photos. He thought that I might reshoot his locales in their present incarnations and write an accompanying text. My girlfriend of six months, Brittni, and I arranged to rent an apartment for the month, but nothing went quite as planned.

With a secret dread of the intimacy of travel growing in both of us, Brittni and I had an argument that began over her check for half of the rent bouncing and elevated quickly to general character assessments, etched in acid, not to be taken back. By the end of the evening she was packing a suitcase while I accompanied the procedure with an impromptu speech, concerning how delighted I was at her departure.

Nothing very elevating on either side was said or done. Nothing one likes to think about on a cross-Atlantic flight. And the end result was that I was alone when I climbed the four flights to my tiny apartment.

Many people had said to me, Oh, you get a month alone in Paris, how marvelous! You'll be walking on air the whole time! But a month alone in a foreign city can be a trying thing. I was twenty-eight, and used to being on my own when need be. I had been to Paris before and knew my way around pretty well. I liked Paris, but didn't love it, and won't ooh and ahh here. There were things I enjoyed, but I wasn't walking on air. I did explore some of the Doisneau sites, but realized the idea was half-baked at best (Doisneau depends on people, not sites), and after a few days I spent most of my time in the *Musee D'Orsay*. I strolled alone along the Seine through the city's lingering dusks, watching elegiac veils of twilight drifting across the gray river and formal gray facades. I left my camera at the apartment.

My French was passable, what I called my Chicago French—forthright, no-frills, utilitarian if not quite brutish. The French waiters' outraged ears might recoil, but they could not deny that they understood me, and so grudgingly brought me what I needed, and even gave me an ounce of respect. Still, our sparring wore on me.

I liked the Marais, where my apartment was. It was a funky, energetic neighborhood, with falafel stands, and cafes that spilled people at all hours. It had the Musee Picasso, a hushed pocket park around the block, and a synagogue by Guimard. It had ephemeral art galleries full of mannequins with submachine guns and saxophones, or imaginary body parts on supper plates.

There was a distractingly beautiful French girl whom I would pass on the stairway. She had a long, elegant, Eleanor of Aquitaine face and light hair, but darting dark eyes. She would bestow on me the gift of her glance and a dulcet, discreet *bon jour*, and then disappear down the twist of the hall. Our apartments shared a wall. I'd also pass in the hallway her surly, unhealthy-looking boyfriend, with slicked-back hair, a sleek, handsome face, and pissed-off eyes. He'd pass me at irregular hours, wearing his boots and leather jacket, like an English Teddyboy from the '50s.

One night I heard them arguing through the wall. He was berating her for sitting with her friends at a café and, he thought, laughing at him as he passed. I listened with every molecule in my brain, madly translating.

Then came a slap and a pained gasp. Another slap and gasp. The sound of sobs.

No translation necessary. His voice raged low. She whimpered. As he talked on his voice turned plaintive, solicitous, reasonable. She murmured meek assent.

The next day she scurried by me, mouse-like, in the hallway.

I'd find discarded hypodermic needles in the gutters outside my building. One day I lifted a tomato on my salad to discover a gob of saliva neatly waiting for me. I called over the waiter, a small man with a sharp face and eyes that seemed to spin with calculation and irony. He was shocked, shocked. I demanded to speak to the manager. My not-quite-crappy French wasn't up to scathing indignation. There were apologies. Though not enough of them.

In short I was lonely and my heart was still smarting from my break up with Brittni. The Parisians seemed cynical, crabby, avaricious. I still had three weeks to go. With what native American pluck I possessed, I decided on the course of self-improvement. I found an advertisement for French lessons at the back of a newspaper. One of those singing French voices answered, an urbane but friendly-sounding woman, and we arranged to meet.

Madame Lili Leblanc lived half-a-dozen Metro stops away, off the *Rue du Faubourg St. Antoine* in the eleventh arrondisement. I got off at the *Faidherbe Chaligny* stop and found *Rue de Ste Jeanne sans Peur*, a short quiet street graced with tall sycamores that muffled what traffic noise there was and broke and sifted the sun. The facades of the apartment buildings contained that signature French combination of formality, softened with a few grace notes—in an architectural whimsy of dolphin lintels or lion-headed doorknockers. Flowers trimmed the somber facades, plants gushed from balconies. I browsed the shop windows full of African masks or musical instruments or antique maps offering tawny, mysterious lands. School girls in tartan skirts and knee socks ran by, their bookbags bouncing on their shoulders.

So it was with a curious, optimistic frame of mind that I rang the bell and was buzzed up by Madame Leblanc. The lobby had a hushed art deco décor, with metal glinting in soft shadows. I took the elevator to the *deuxieme étage* and walked to the end of a carpeted hallway where a door stood open a few inches. I knocked uncertainly, pushing the door open a few more inches, and the pretty little triangle of a face poked out.

"Russell?" She gave the R a subtle, guttural trill.

"Madame Leblanc?"

"Yes. Come in."

The front room of her apartment, all in pastel tints, gave the impression of luxe et calme, and of space used with unflagging efficiency. One wall consisted entirely of books, CDs, and records, and another was a five-paneled, sliding-doored closet with a nicely done mural of a Provencal landscape. There was a sun-flushed balcony full of plants over-looking the street below. In the three weeks of our daily lessons, never did I see anything out of place. Never was a stray jacket thrown over a chair or a pile of books collapsed on the divan.

Without ado, she sat me at a small desk, sat across from me, and we began. She was a short, trim woman, maybe fifty, wearing a peach blouse and dark skirt, quite attractive, with that secretive, cat-like face that French women somehow contrived for themselves. Her eyelids were perpetually lowering slowly to cover half her smoky-green iris, as if withdrawing into herself for further contemplation. Then she would slowly open them as she would begin to reveal to you what she had discovered in there.

Since she seemed to know no more than a few dozen English words, we spoke only in French. I felt my disadvantage quickly. I could understand her French pretty well, but could only respond at about a sixth-grade level, and after maybe ten minutes of preliminaries, I was receiving an exegesis on American's sins and character flaws. Vietnam, Nicaragua, nuclear winter, the CIA.

I'm no Yankee chauvinist, and I agreed with many of her criticisms, but I was always thinking, yes, but, yes, but. And she suffered no buts. It was only wrong, wrong, wrong. So I took the bait.

"Whenever countries have power, they've abused it. France would do the same. They would be no better."

"No! No! Russell, you must listen to me! You are wrong! France has learned its lesson in Algeria. We would never be so arrogant. It would be better for the world if Russia won the Cold War!"

"Please, Madame Leblanc. Listen to yourself."

"Russia is stupid too. You are right. But this *Pax Americana*. If only there were *Pax*! You are like the Romans. Cruel, arrogant, stupid. I do not mean you, personally, of course. You are a very nice person. I mean only people like you."

If you've ever been immersed in a foreign language, you know that after a certain point, your brain becomes a sponge that can absorb no more. The brain recoils. Whatever part of your consciousness still remains runs away into a little cottage in the woods far back in your mind, crawls into bed and pulls the covers over its head.

"You are perhaps tired?" she said at last, and we agreed to stop and to meet again the next day. I wasn't fond of the hail of abuse, but I had to admit my French was improving, if only out of self-defense.

At the next lesson, Madame Leblanc said, "You know many words, but people will never understand you. You sound as if you are from Texas! Yes, you sound like a Texas cowboy!" She chuckled to herself. "A Texas cowboy! Yes. So much like John Wayne! No, this will not do. You must read to me out loud. We will give you our verbal calisthenics! Never known to fail!"

So we fell into a pattern in our lessons in which I would read out loud to her from some of the French classics, and she would correct my pronunciation. We would always leave about twenty-minutes of my daily hour for random conversation. It turned out that not only did foreign policy fill the thinking hours of Madame Leblanc, but she could also inform me about American culture and domestic affairs.

"We do not have slums like yours. You treat your minorities as if they were not human!"

Well, the conditions are terrible, but...a political stalemate...occasional progress...I stuttered...and the Arabs here.

"The Arabs are treated like everyone else. Some of them, they do not wish to work."

"Have you ever been to the States?" I tried.

"Yes!" she parried. "I spent a week in New York City and walked everywhere and saw everything. It was exhilarating. I do not hate all things American. I love John Lee Hooker. Miles Davis. Sam Cooke." She rattled off the names. "They are not, of course, real Americans." She gave me her knowing, somnolent cat look. "They are blacks."

But...

"Your movies are everywhere!" she said. "So vulgar! So stupid. *The French Connection*. What did that movie mean? That we are all drug dealers?"

Well, but...you see...Hollywood....

And so we argued, if my primitive sentences could be called arguments at all. She was Porthos, elegant in kneeboots and cape, swishing her rapier as she paced around the hapless rube who had crossed her somehow, and whom she now and then gave a lightning jab. There seemed to be an invisible crowd watching us. Madame Leblanc seemed to hear silent cheers as the Gauls triumphed.

In our readings we sampled Diderot, Verlaine, Stendhal, Proust.

"There's an elegance that all these writers tend to have in common," I noted.

"Yes," she said. "It is good that you notice that. You are an American but you are not stupid." For a moment she pondered this conundrum. "You do not quite understand." She stood up. Our lesson was over for the day. "But almost."

After a week my hazing was over. Madame Leblanc had addressed my various areas of ignorance and let history, foreign policy, race relations, and cultural critiques take a back seat to literature and to more personal conversations.

She told me that she had been a child during the war. Because her father was Jewish they fled to Algeria, where she lived for six years. Yes, she was a *pied-noire*, like Camus. She still remembered the boat ride across the Mediterranean, the tears of her mother. It was not a pleasure cruise.

And her father! Of course even during the war he had to make money or else they would starve. Involved in the black market, twice he snuck back to the German sector, was twice captured by the Germans, and twice escaped. Once he was held on a long bench at a railway station with other prisoners, guarded by a callow youth in an ill-fitting uniform, just a boy, who walked up and down the station's platform. Each time the guard turned his back, her father edged closer to the edge of the bench. Finally he slipped off the bench and around the building into the darkness. He followed the railroad south. It took him two months to find his way back to Algeria and his family. "He knew how to survive," she said tersely. "He was not a nurturing man. But he knew what it took to survive."

"And the war took its toll on me! Look at me!" She stood up and twirled around. "Look at me! I am deformed!"

"No," I protested.

"Yes! But yes! My hands and feet are large." She thrust her hands before my face. "Look! Look! But I am so short! It is because of malnutrition during the war! The Boches did this to me! That is why I thought I would never marry."

She seemed delighted by the thought of the dirty Boches, exile in Algeria, and malnutrition, and twirled around again, her skirt lifting like a figureskater's.

Lili was a good teacher and my French improved, my accent, speed, and comprehension. I got our lessons down on a pocket taperecorder and later played back her lilting voice, trying to engrave her pronunciation in my mind. As I walked the streets or rode the Metro, exchanges that had once been sonic blurs to me popped clearly into meaning. I began to look forward to our conversations and would come along the *Rue de Ste. Jeanne Sans Peur*, browse the windows full of African masks or antique maps, and look up to the third floor balcony where Madame Leblanc's plants were a green blaze. Sometimes she would be out watering them and would look down and wave gaily to me.

One day we were reading the episode in *Swann's Way* in which Swann, in a frenzy of jealousy, searches through café after café for Odette, his wayward lover, and each time he scans another room for her face in vain, his anguish grows. Finally, in black despair, he gives up, and returns down the darkening boulevard. And then, as if conjured by his own dejection, no, it can't be, it was Odette walking toward him out of the dusk, like Eurydice returned from the land of the dead, smiling, innocent.

Madame Leblanc put out her hand and covered the book from which I read. The passage had saddened her.

She gave me a grave look and said, "Once, for several minutes, I was dead."

"What do you mean?"

"I have a very bad heart, you see, and they gave me this operation. Open-hearted surgery, it is called," she said, unhappily attempting a rare English phrase. "The French doctors, they are very good. The best in the world. And our insurance, too, the best. Your insurance, ooh-lala. We laugh at it. But even the best doctors cannot guarantee everything. My heart, it stops. For seven hours only machines keep me alive. That too is its own death. And afterwards, for a few minutes, they say, something went wrong. Now I am changed. I know what nothingness is like."

"You must be grateful for every day," I said. What could I say, after such a revelation?

"No. You are wrong, Russell. It is not simple like that. Americans think everything is simple. Even alive now, hm? Even now, I know what it is like to have a dead heart, eh? Eh?"

"What do you mean?"

"Oh, I am depressing today. I do not want to depress you. I tell you stories about myself. But you never tell me stories about yourself."

"No. I don't like to talk about myself."

"But you are the one who is supposed to be talking!"

I shrugged.

"Do you know what nothingness is like, Russell?" she asked. "To live with the nothingness? To be dunked into an icy black pool like ink, eh?"

I thought for a moment. "I know things can be bittersweet," I said. "Even the best of things."

The French term, *amerdoux*, lets you feel both tastes on your tongue as you say it. Her eyes lit up.

"Yes! Yes! You understand! Life is bittersweet! It is *amerdoux*. You and me, Russell, we understand things the same. We are precisely the same."

One day when I arrived for my lesson, I met Madame Leblanc's husband, who was departing on a trip. He had carried two bulky leather suitcases into the center of the room and stood precisely between them, as if poised at a starter's gate. He was a short, handsome man with a lush Elvis forelock swoop and sideburns. We shook hands. He couldn't have cared less, his edgy eyes roving away even as we shook, his mind elsewhere, rabbiting around the room. He dropped my hand and strode to a desk to retrieve some documents, stuffed them in his jacket pocket, exchanging rapid-fire sentences with Lili. Both of their actions and voices were calm, but they seemed, beneath the surface, somehow agitated. Lili took leave of him at the door. He was, I knew, a nuclear engineer who worked in the nuclear power industry and traveled frequently, much sought after overseas for his expertise and international charm.

"Your husband seems nice," I told Madame Leblanc when we were seated again at our desk, where I'd grown to feel quite at home, ready for the lesson to begin. It was what one said, so I said it. But he didn't seem nice. He seemed vain and self-absorbed.

"Yes," Madame Leblanc agreed. "Yes. Everyone loves my husband."

She had me begin to read aloud some poetry, correcting my pronunciation as we went. Then: "My husband," she interrupted me, "is going to Russia with a co-worker for two weeks."

"Oh?"

"Yes. This co-worker...." Madame paused. "You see, she is a young woman." Madame gave me her slow, cat-eyed, significant look, the lids dipping and rising. "Everyone loves my husband. Especially the young women."

"Oh!"

"But continue! Continue your reading!"

I read for a while without correction, till I began to hear my own grating pronunciation. Usually her corrections were swift and merciless, but today she was letting me slip into my John Wayne drawl without a wince.

"Are you sad?" I finally asked, lowering the book.

"No." She shook her head determinedly. "No. I am accustomed to it. I am lonely perhaps. But not sad because of my husband's behavior. Continue! Continue to read!"

I lifted the book. She said, "You have had, perhaps, some sadness in your life."

"Some," I said. "Enough for my taste."

"I can see that. I can see that in your face."

"Oh."

I didn't like that someone could see anything in my face that I didn't want them to see. But if anyone was to see it, it might as well be Lili.

"You look to me like an Italian."

"But I'm not dark."

"No, like a northern Italian. I have seen men who look like you in Milan."

"Oh." I took my sudden un-American appearance in Lili's eyes as a promotion of sorts.

Nearing the end of our last week of lessons, Lili greeted me dressed in a crimson scarf, a gray pleated skirt and yellow jersey. "Today," she said, "I have planned an outing. Yes, we will go somewhere special."

We descended to the basement of her apartment building, where she had an old bug-eyed Citroen, the style that seemed to demand Bogart in a raincoat as driver. We clambered aboard. Her feet scarcely reached the pedals. "I do not drive much," she said. With a spastic jerk of the clutch, we rocketed out of the basement and onto the street. We were off on Mr. Toad's Wild Ride.

At the intersection she lurched to a halt before an unending line of cars, then, with a thrusting of bumpers and profusion of honks, she wedged the Citroën into a gap between two cars, the product of someone's split-second hesitation. In a few blocks we were on a massive multi-lane roundabout, circling a monument to some Gallic bloodletting. Around and around we went in dizzying circles. "The French, the French are the worst of all," she muttered cryptically, but a moment later, "*Sales gosses!*" she shouted at a carload of dusky youths in her path, "Go back to Algeria!"

With doomed, crackling laughter, she pulled hard on the steering wheel—a mariner against the typhoon—shot across three lanes of traffic, swerved off on a tangent, swung a right into a street so narrow we dusted flanks of cars on either side, hooked another corner where we confronted a ramshackle pickup truck, loaded with bulging crates of lettuce, barreling toward us.

"*Un bordel complet!*"

She screeched to a halt, oblivious to the truck's windshield full of shrieking faces, and executed a lightning maneuver in reverse.

As in the inexplicable transitions of dreams, we next found ourselves on a sleek, empty road, cruising in silence. I took a breath. We glided into a parking lot next to a seventeenth-century mansion, parked, and stepped onto the logical, bosky grounds. "This is my favorite park," Lili said. We strolled around the mansion and down a magisterial staircase, by an oblong pool with a line of conch-blowing mermen, and then off on a path of crunching pebbles through the rhododendrons.

As we walked, Lili, usually so precise in her movements, kept bumping into me, knocking my thigh with her hip, brushing my hand with hers, somehow bumping her breast into my side.

We found a bench in a niche overlooking a smaller pool, and sat, thigh to thigh. Looked out over the pool. "This is a special place for me," she said. "I have never brought anyone here with me before you. You are the first."

"Oh," I said primly. "Thank you."

She turned to look at me. Suddenly both of her hands shot out and fluffed my hair. "There. That is better." She tilted her heart-shaped face toward me. I gave her a cretinous grin. Looked out over the pool some more. A leaf swirled on the surface.

I did not want this, I thought. Although I'd felt a growing affection for Lili, she wasn't my type. She was fifty and I was twenty-eight. No, this would never do. I would just wait it out. I would be the most oblivious, obtuse American ever to cross the Atlantic.

She prattled for awhile about the park, about a storm that had decimated the trees several years before.

Then a stagnant pool of silence grew between us. I let it grow. And grow.

Finally, after a long, dispirited look at me, she shook her head and stood to go.

The ride back was a tamer affair and Lili's manic mood had evaporated. The wrinkles around her eyes had deepened so that she looked almost haggard. She sighed as we sat in traffic, as if it were pointless to ever go anywhere.

"You people," she said, as I left that day. "You can be very nice, you go to the moon, but certain things you will never understand."

The next day was muggy and overcast, the day of my last lesson, one day before I was to fly to New York. In an autumnal mood, I took the Metro and walked down the *Rue de Ste. Jeanne Sans Peur*. Lili must've felt something of the same mood, because we dragged our way through the lessons listlessly. What more was I going to learn in one day? What did anything matter? Wasn't life just one bitter disappointment after another? A heavy Frankish-pessimism filled the air and poisoned the mood.

After precisely an hour she reached across the desk and shut the book from which I was reading, patted my hand once.

"It is time?" I asked.

"Yes, Russell, it is time."

"Then this is good-bye."

"Yes."

We stood up.

"Good-bye." She stretched out her hand for me to shake, her arm at full-length,.

I shook her hand. "I might be back in Paris next year." This was a new idea. I had no reason to believe that it was true.

"Oh, yes? Come and see me then."

"I will."

"We can begin our lessons again."

"I look forward to it."

"You will perhaps then learn how to say '*oreille*' correctly."

"Someday."

She walked me to the door and I stepped into the hallway. She peeked her little heart-shaped catface in the crack of the door. Her face glowed with a tender melancholy. "*Au revoir*, Russell."

"*Au revoir.*"

I turned to go.

A last reluctant tumbler clicked into place, springing open some lock inside me.

I whirled back, executing a decent pointguard's pivot-fake.

"Lili?" She had already turned away from the door. Just as she turned back at my call, in my eagerness to catch her I pushed the door: it caught her smack in the face. She stumbled back, holding her nose.

"Oh!" A pained cry.

I stepped back into the room and she gave me a reproachful look over her hand, still on her nose. She took her hand away, inspecting it with interest. Blood was flowing from both nostrils. She plucked at some tissues on the desk, rushed to the kitchen, her hand cupped to her face. I followed her and stood by the sink, apologizing and making irrelevant offers of help while she leaned back her head, pressing a dampened dishtowel to her nose.

She gave me a long, appraising look.

"You are strange," she concluded.

"I suppose so," I confessed. "It's lamentable."

"And impetuous." She inspected the wadded towel. "Better now," she said.

Impetuous and strange, I took her by both elbows and pulled her to me and kissed her on the mouth, her upper lip still damp from the towel. When I let her go she said, "I have always bled easily at the nose. You must learn to be more gentle."

"Yes," I said.

We kissed again, and she led me to her bedroom, a small, twilit room, mostly filled by the white, chenille-covered bed, where two dry-cleaned suits lay crisscrossed like ghostly lovers. Lili picked up the suits and hung them in the closet with a business-like air that belied a shakiness to her movements. Funny, how sex combines the matter-of-fact with the mysterious, so it feels as if our little bodies aren't quite up to the task of containing all our contradictions and billowing emotions.

"Look," she said, stopping by the window. "It is raining." We stood together, taking in the rustling of the leaves and the cool scent of rain. She shivered and half-closed the windows, paced down the narrow space between the bed and the window, like a bird discovering itself caged, thrashing for an exit, turned about, bumped against me as if surprised to find me there, kissed me, and then abruptly sat on the bed.

She removed her blouse, snapped off her bra with an angular motion, and, arms crossed over her breasts, looked at me. I sat next to her and kissed her along the neck. When she turned to me, letting her arms fall, the scar from her heart operation showed, a lightning bolt ripping between her breasts, so much worse than I had imagined, that I had to stop myself from gasping or staring. But my reaction showed in the way I averted my gaze.

"It is not too lovely, is it?" she said, eyes smiling, mouth serious.

"No." She took my hand and led it to the scar. I ran my finger down the cicatrix, ragged and puckered on the edges, but smooth as melted glass to the touch.

"One must crack open the breastbone, to reach the heart," she said, trembling slightly, and lying back on the bed. "It is a very difficult operation, to reach the heart."

"Yes," I said. "Yes, it is."

The rain tambourined on the sycamore leaves, gradually slowing. A low-angled sun broke through. The Catholic school up the street let out, and the voices of children rose to us. Gradually the room grew dark and our bodies seemed to shimmer with a phosphorescence. We showered and dressed and crossed the street to the *brasserie* on the corner. The rain had brought down bundles of the sycamore leaves, large as napkins, plastering them to the sidewalks where they left a rusty stain, bright in the sharp circle of streetlights. Lili knew the waiters but was unabashed at being seen with me, the illicit one, holding my hand as we ordered, and greeted one of her neighbors, a courtly man with a cranky Scot's terrier straining his leash. She introduced me as her *cher ami*, Russell, thrilling me with that guttural, erotic trill she gave to the R in my name.

Back at her apartment we made love again and then we'd sleep for awhile and then dream and wake up making love and then sleep some more. I remember in the middle of the night, socked into a pocket of rare trust, I'd told Lili about the death of my father a year before, things I'd never told Brittni. She told me about being a child in Algiers, where she ran barefoot rolling a hoop with a stick through the streets and ran helterskelter through the marketplace with the Arab children. Later in the war, there was so little food that no one had the energy to run, and they sat around on dusty stoops or stayed home and listened to American jazz on the radio. When she came to Paris after the war it was still a time of great poverty but also hope. She remembered seeing Sartre and Beauvoir in the *Café de Flore* and the brash confidence that they exuded.

We woke late the next morning. It was ten and I had a flight at noon. She gave me a ride to my apartment and watched while I packed, willynilly throwing clothes into suitcases, while she stood in the doorway nodding her head as if in fond approval or confirmation of what I'll never know. She drove me out to Charles DeGaulle and it was good bye. She tipped up her happy cat face to kiss me and cinched her arms tightly about my neck for just a brief moment. On the flight back to Kennedy, I thought I might be more than a little in love with Madame Lili Leblanc.

Within twenty-four hours of landing at JFK, I'd been had, ripped off, or fooled three times. Groggy, jet-lagged, sad, I wasn't on guard. First, I followed an unlicensed cabby who came up to me as I retrieved my luggage, led me into a parking lot, and then took off sprinting as airport security came to meet us. Next, I let myself be persuaded by the genuine limo driver to share my ride as he billed double fares. Finally, with Bronx brass, with his angry dismay at the couple of bucks I gave him, he guilted and browbeat me into overtipping him. Welcome home. Hurrah for the red-white-and-blue. The next day as I emerged from the subway, five or six kids rushed by me, one snatching my backpack, hanging loosely from my shoulder. They took off hurtling down the street. I'd grown dreamy and soft in the elegant arms of Paris.

Within six weeks I was back with Brittni, and within eight months we had married. Lili and I exchanged a number of letters over the next year or so, not *billets-doux,* certainly—maybe *billets-amerdoux.* After a time these trailed off, and the rush of daily events crowded out the memory of Lili.

Let me say this about Brittni, though our marriage didn't last long and this story isn't about her. She was a model, a natural blonde, a sliver under six-feet tall, with an angular face that the camera loved to caress along its fine edges. I think beneath her beauty and her assertiveness (she was given to bold gestures) she was often terrified, and expected me to calm those terrors. But she was frantic where I was casual, shakey where I was convinced. Each of us was pointed where the other was tender. She zigged when I zagged. Her subterranean fears made her tyrannical on trivial points, so I walked each day through a series of boobytraps. Though we tried to love each other in our clumsy way, I found I'd traded a certain honesty in my day-to-day actions for the illusions projected on her glamour. Soon it was a relief to be alone after a day with her. Soon we were both doing and saying things whose memory will stop you in your tracks years later.

It wasn't until three years had passed, with my divorce in its last legal throes, that I found myself back in Paris, this time only for three days before I was to take the overnight train to Rome. On my first day I found myself just a Metro stop away from the *Rue de Ste Jeanne Sans Peur*, and decided to surprise Lili, hopping on the train smiling to myself, anticipating various scenarios of reunion. I was eager to see her, not to renew a love affair, but because I felt I'd betrayed my better self when I'd married, and I was hoping Lili would help restore a clearer sense of that other person, the one I'd planned on being.

I took the familiar stroll beneath the sycamores, with their bark peeling in patches to form a camouflage pattern, down *Rue de Ste Jeanne Sans Peur*, glancing up to Lili's patio. It was barren of her plants that had used to fill the space with a plush green.

I pushed the buzzer to her apartment number six and waited what seemed like a long time. A harsh, small, female voice answered my buzz. Hearing my accent, the woman switched immediately to rawly accented English: "I do not know of this Madame Leblanc."

A man's voice in the background was asking, repeatedly, "*Qui est la? Qui est la?*"

The woman rudely shushed him. "Good bye now," she said to me. "Okay?"

There was a silence as I stood there. Then I heard a minute electrical click as the woman pushed the button again to talk. "You there? You mean the woman who used to live here? Yes? She has suffered a crisis cardiac now and has died." The man was interrupting her again in the background. "That is what happened then, all right? Please go away now."

Dazed, gutshot, I turned and walked away, to the end of the street and then down *Rue de St. Antoine*.

I should have called. I should have written, I thought. But mostly I didn't think, I just kept walking. Sometimes I became momentarily aware of my surroundings and would find myself in a crowd of shoppers among bins of cheap flipflops and plastic handbags. Or suddenly, as if transported, beside a highway rushing like a river. I let myself become absorbed into the venerable streets of the city.

Much later I found myself again on Lili's street, ineluctably drawn to glance again at the balcony, bereft of plants, to look again at the blank next to her buzzer, stifling an impulse to ring for her again, like a child who can't accept that a playmate has moved away. But I wandered on past, uncertain where to go.

At the end of the block I sat at a sidewalk table and ordered coffee, brought to me by a lanky, surly waiter. I watched the Catholic schoolgirls pass, in their same plaid skirts, white blouses, and knee socks—different girls, undoubtedly. The original girls had moved on. But not me.

I differed with my friend, my lover, Lili, on her concept of nothingness, because an obscure sense of being observed replaced that first feeling of stomach-sucking vacuum, a sense diffused up and down the *Rue de Ste. Jeanne Sans Peur*, lingering in the huge leaves of the sycamores or in the almond eyes of the African masks.

Scratch an American, Lili, and you'll find a sentimentalist.

I took out the small, cigarette-pack-sized tape recorder I'd used three years before, pushed the play button, and listened to Lili's voice. She was reciting from memory a Prevert poem.

> *Deux et deux quatre*
> *Quatre et quatre huit....*
> *Mais voila l'oiseau-lyre*
> *Qui passe dans le ciel...*

The waiter was wiping the white metal tables, impatient, I thought, for me to leave, but at the sound of Lili's voice he stopped cold and stared at me.

"You were Lili's friend?" he asked.

"Yes."

"I was, too. Lili, I miss her." *Elle me manque.*

"Me too."

He nodded his head in grave affirmation.

> *"les pupitres redeviennent arbres*
> *la craie redevient falaise*
> *le porte-plume redevient oiseau."*

The poem was about a boy dreaming in a classroom till the scene transformed itself, the desks reverting back into trees, the chalk back into the cliffs, the plume-pen back to the bird from which it had been plucked.

Still listening to Lili's tinny singsong, the waiter began to wipe the tables again, pushing his towel in circles around and around the same spot, smiling ruefully and shaking his head.

~Gutted~

Gregg Cusick

Tuesday, August 3, 1989. 7:03 a.m.

Joseph Dromski gazed upward along the length of the crane, squinting through the already stifling haze. His reddened eyes followed the steel arm to where it reached out over the beams and girders, the skinless skeleton of the skyscraper under construction. He wondered just when it was, and how, he had lost it. "Christ, I'm tired," he said aloud.

It seemed to him that there had been definite events that had caused it. Lost promotions that had gone to less qualified, as favors and payoffs. Jackie running away, what, seven years ago, eight? Joseph could not see the incidents as the skid marks they were, merely warning signs on a long, steadily descending stretch of highway. And he did not wonder how negativity and hatred had replaced their opposites in his life, for it was such a gradual process.

And so it was that he did daily now things unconscionable ten years before, justifying his personal evolution in steps as it paralleled his perception of the world's decline. Each step could be justified from the one preceding it, yet Joseph Dromski had no conception of the huge number of such steps; they ran together in his mind which latched onto only a handful of specific events that must explain, he would tell someone across the bar, the laziness and lack of morality in today's youth or the warring in the Middle East. And so as he stared through the haze at the crane's arm, he tried only to justify the action of the previous step, last night ... Careless, he thought. Stupid kid.

Joseph Dromski watched the crew spreading slowly out over the site, and he, too, moved sluggishly toward the elevator cage. But as it lurched into motion, lifting him over the city, he felt none of the thrill he remembered once feeling. He sometimes saw it now in the eyes of the younger men, and he thought them foolish, unrealistic. Wise up, he sometimes told them (he'd told Teddie). Wake up and smell the coffee, and the burned toast, he'd chuckle, watching their eyes to see if his blows registered.

Tiny sweat droplets formed on his balding head, and inside, the dull throbbing began again. "Christ, it's hot," he told no one in particular.

Joseph looked around the elevator, peering guardedly at the grim faces of the other six riders, men he had known, it seemed, forever. He remembered when their moods were light and easy, and the men looked up to him, quick with a joke and the next round of Pabst. But now they hardly looked. So they're guiltier than I, Joseph took this to mean, and knew that soon he could believe it ... One more step.

The sun sliced through the wire cage and left lined shadows on the gray overalls of the riders. Their clothing now matched their faces, appearing like a prison chain gang.

Monday, August 2, 1989. 5:19 p.m.

Maggie sat on the concrete steps of the brownstone that was like all other brownstones, anywhere, and waved to Ted as he let her father out and drove off. She liked Ted, had dated him from time to time, and he had lately taken to coming into the bar some nights near closing time. Yet after a couple of drinks he would leer like a predator, over-tipping and bragging about "going places." He acted as if he deserved her rather than wanted her, and at times he spoke of life in the cynical terms he had learned from her father. Jackie had escaped before he could be so influenced, yet Teddie seemed sometimes to lap it up so eagerly. What were they doing in the middle of these nights, she wondered.

"You look like a hooker on the corner of Rush," she heard her father say. You should know, Maggie thought, not meeting his eyes. "Find a sailor to slap you around a little, huh?" And he was past her and into the building.

Yet the remarks no longer drew blood as they once had, as when Jackie had first left. Maggie silently prayed that this was not because she was drained like her mother, an embalmed body in which no blood remained. She thought again of Teddie, who was apparently unaware that he, too, was losing blood to this man.

Maggie remained on the steps, listening, as her father heavily climbed the wooden steps inside, angrily but without the energy to be. Bitter.

Joseph Dromski entered the kitchen his wife had made even hotter by using the oven. Without a word he took a beer from the refrigerator and slumped into the leather-cracked stuffed chair in the front room. He unbuttoned the straps of the gray overalls, revealing a sleeveless tee-shirt sweat-stained the color of his teeth.

"Do you think you might sometime serve something *cool* in weather like this?" he called toward the doorway, switching on the television to drown her possible answer.

But she offered none, only acknowledging another check on a mental calendar, another day unchanged. Della had felt her energy, her life in these past years, escaping in tiny wisps, sucked out through the door that each evening he reentered. More and more it seemed locked from the outside behind him.

He used to tell her it was she who had changed, but recently he had begun telling her the opposite—that change was demanded and she had not. "You've got to modify," he'd say. "You've got to get tough."

"They'll kill us, Del," he used to tell her, before he had modified. Before he began working nights and talking less.

And Maggie told her not to listen, to take the blows and think of her own dreams, of returning to teaching, or just getting out. But Della did not sleep well, and her dreams she tried not to remember.

She, too, wondered how and why so much had been lost. She did not understand the steps involved, could not trace it. I still miss Jackie, she thought. If I could get past that, I know I'd be better for Joseph. "He's takin' you, Ma," she heard her son, could it be eight years ago, "surer than if he was beatin' you with his fists ..." Thank God, at least, for that, she had thought at the time. Yet now, as she held the counter, the nauseating emptiness warm inside her, she was not so sure.

"Do you work again tonight?" Della asked, calling over the television, spooning chicken casserole onto a faded china plate, its blue flowered design worn unrecognizable. He did not answer, and as she handed him the meal his eyes did not leave the screen.

Maggie remained on the front steps, listening to the television news pouring from the second floor window and thinking of her mother. Finally she rose and checked her watch, knowing she would be early for work.

Tuesday, August 3, 1989. 2:12 a.m.

Joseph Dromski awoke with a start as the filter of the cigarette held loosely between his fingers seared his knuckles. He swore under his breath and stared across the room, completely disoriented. Worn furniture was bathed in blue-gray radiation light emitted from the silent television. Joseph stared blearily through the smoke at the small rectangle of light in which Groucho Marx was miming "You Bet Your Life." The emcee handed a schoolteacher from Iowa fifty dollars for using the word attached to the foot of a suspended duck. ". . . a common household word, something you see every day," Joseph mocked thickly. And then all was silent again save for an occasional passing vehicle on the still stifling street outside.

Joseph Dromski glanced at his watch now and rose quickly. He found his work boots lying neatly beside the door and mechanically tugged the laces through eyelets, pulling them tight as his hockey skates decades ago. He did not hear his wife breathing unevenly in the bedroom whose door stood ajar.

If we could finish this place tonight, he thought as he closed the door and slipped down the wooden stairs, maybe I could get some sleep. Yet as he stepped out into the moonless August night, he was wide awake, his mind actively calculating.

It had been a fine old building, 1920 maybe, and if the yard man believed even older, the bricks could sell for at least twenty-eight cents apiece. At least twenty-two hundred in the truck meant he could cut Teddie his seventy-five—for two hours work, more than I ever made at his age, the ingrate—and still have, what, five hundred plus in his pocket. That would buy a long nap, and maybe an afternoon at Arlington with the ponies.

The truck turned over grudgingly on the second try—the damn

thing runs better in a Chicago winter, he thought—and Joseph drove slowly toward the south side, not worried that Teddie may have waited as he overslept. He'll get paid, Dromski told the rearview mirror, nodding at the deserted streets.

Behind him in the brownstone, Della Dromski lit a cigarette and sat up in bed, feeling somehow better the moment the door closed behind him. Endurance seemed the only goal on nights like this.

Yet it had not always been this way, she counseled herself again. She remembered the winter nights watching from behind the glass as he glided over the ice so swift and full of boyish determination. And then the breezeless summer nights like this one, passing back and forth warm pints of beer on a blanket by the lake. Watching the barge silhouettes far away and the stars. Kissing, laughing. High school, she thought. And then the wedding and the Army and the children and still, she thought, they had been happy. Yet somehow, she could not place exactly when, it stopped feeling the same.

It was partially now, Della thought, that dammit she still loved the man. And partially her upbringing, for her mother would never have imagined leaving her father, whose drinking bouts and violence were much more common than her own Joseph's. She had taught Della perseverance and preached forgiveness, always forgiveness, and as Della did now, had often blamed herself. And when Maggie pleaded with her to get out, she could never muster the strength to abandon that boy on the blanket by the lake so long since gone.

Della Dromski rose, stubbing out her cigarette, and entered the warm kitchen. With resolve she began laying out bread and mustard and sliced ham, the ritual and the mere motion of it a comfort.

She could not continue to hear the voices of Maggie and Jackie in one ear, and Joseph in the other. Her love went out to both sides, yet she was torn and unsettled.

Della listened to the steady, scuffing beat of the ancient coffee percolator. Outside, a car engine neared and quieted. She heard Maggie's footsteps on the stairs, and looked up to see the front room an eerie blue-gray as the television played on silently without audience. She turned back to her work.

Tuesday, August 3, 1989. 2:37 a.m.

Maggie closed the door quietly, wearily, and saw her mother's back to her at the counter, bread laid out in neat rows before her. She knew her entrance had been heard, and moved behind her mother, kissed her cheek.

"Take these over to . . ." her mother began, then stopped, thinking *My God, that was just like* him, and tried to smile. "Honey, how did it go tonight?"

Della felt suddenly defensive, not wanting her daughter to say a word. Embarrassed to be making him sandwiches in the middle of the night. She turned her head slightly so that Maggie's words might be channeled into her right ear, Joseph's ear.

Maggie loved her mother, and she knew what her mother had begun to ask. She understood her, and part of her loved the unfinished order. Was this where she was different from Jackie, she wondered, and more like this woman at the counter?

Yet the part of Maggie that did not love this "slip" by her mother, the unanswered love her action represented, the weakness . . . this part of Maggie hated her father, suddenly and deeply. She realized this feeling had existed for as long as she could remember. Jackie, she thought, help me now.

Maggie had watched her father gouge into people as his own self-hatred went unacknowledged. She felt him trying to take from her all that was inside her, because he had relinquished all that was inside himself. And she had watched him take away her mother's self-respect and her dreams, almost laughing that it was so easy.

Maggie had watched this since her youth, and had found her mother in tears, or worse, like this now, many times. And she had been there to comfort her. But did she respect her mother for taking all this—for letting him destroy her because he felt wronged? Part of Maggie despised this weakness in her mother and in herself.

Maggie hesitated. "I'll run the sandwiches over to Daddy," she said. "I'm still wired from work, could use the air. I know the area they're working—Teddie told me the other night." Her mother looked up seriously.

They stared at each other for a moment. Della's eyes sought an answer, what two construction workers could be doing in the middle of the night. Then, Maggie thought, they seemed to dart, to withdraw the question.

"I love you, Mom," Maggie said simply, pouring hot coffee into the thermos.

Tuesday, August 3, 1989. 3:21 a.m.

Joseph Dromski waited by the truck in near-total blackness, sweating. He saw no lights on in the apartment building opposite the abandoned brick structure where he stood, and no sign of human life at all on the other sides, a small park and a dusty, littered vacant lot. Ted emerged from the condemned building, his shirt perspiration soaked, pushing the wheelbarrow laden with clay-colored bricks.

"That's got to be about it," Teddie panted. Joseph frowned, seeing room in the pickup for maybe, he quickly calculated, seventy more.

"A few more," said Joseph Dromski, looking at the truck.

"The interior walls . . ." Teddie began, frustrated, catching his breath. ". . .shouldn't try," he attempted, faltering, knowing it was dangerous to spark Joseph's short fuse.

As Joseph helped him stack the bricks into the bed of the truck, Ted knew that he would reenter the gutted structure. Joseph finally stood still and waited, as Teddie lifted the wheelbarrow the last time.

"Greedy bastard," Ted muttered under his breath, cursing more himself, for a lifetime of yielding in this game of chicken. He rolled the cart through the doorless entryway and into complete darkness.

Tuesday, August 3, 1989. 3:29 a.m.

Maggie had passed and rounded the same block twice before she recognized her father's truck. In the blackness it was barely visible beneath the structure that stood, she could tell, without glass in the windows or occupancy of anything but pigeons and rats.

Her Volkswagen stalled, the engine dying, as she saw the barrel-like form of her father and the tall, massless skeleton of Teddie pushing a wheelbarrow. The men exchanged words, but in the silence from a block away she could not make them out. What were they doing?

There was a moment, then, of total absolute silence, which Maggie thought she had been granted to understand something. Something you already knew, Jackie would tell her. But as she watched Teddie reenter the hollow structure she thought, I've missed it.

It was not, she would think later, violent or deafening, even played upon the background of complete silence. It was soundless, like a film she suddenly remembered seeing in grade school, of an earthquake somewhere out west. Buildings fell this way, she remembered thinking. Without narration or description; without emotion.

The last brick . . .

And then she remembered Teddie, as three of the exterior walls of the building in slow motion collapsed upon each other like a house of cards. The coffee in the thermos on the seat beside her remained hot.

Maggie turned the key and the car sputtered. The engine caught. She sat for a moment comforted, concentrating on this low rumbling, grateful. And she spun the car around, in the rearview mirror seeing the figure of her father leap into the cab of the truck. She accelerated, screeching around one corner and hitting the lights, stopping only when she felt out of reach and the telephone booth appeared in her path.

She was quite calm with the police, she thought later. Speaking evenly and giving no names, saying please just send an ambulance quickly I know nothing more. And just as calmly and rationally she somehow knew there was no hope. He has taken from Teddie what he took from Momma, and me, and God knows who else. What he took from the building itself . . . and we will all eventually collapse, she thought, our insides looted but the facades left apparently unblemished, betraying no damage.

Maggie packed quickly, leaving a note in her mother's handbag, nothing more than Jackie's address. Yet she knew her mother could not follow her now.

As the first streaks of hazy light appeared in the rearview mirror, Maggie saw the silhouette of the city, the skyscrapers rising proudly from the darkness beneath. And only then did the tears begin to fill her eyes and fall silently onto the work shirt she had never changed. There was something different about these tears, she thought, for they were not shed and lost in the night to be found again the next. They meant something, for they came with motion, and change. She gripped the wheel tightly, staring straight ahead.

Tuesday, August 3, 1989. 7:18 a.m.

The elevator cage stopped at the top of the city, and the man closest to the gate hesitated a moment before sliding it aside. And it seemed to Joseph Dromski that the shadows of prison stripes remained on the overalls of the seven men long after they had stepped out into the sun. "Christ, it's hot," he said.

~Catapult~

Emily Fridlund

That summer I was reading vampire books, so when Noah said no to sex, I let myself pretend that's what he was. I told myself: inside his mouth is a hallway to death. That's why his teeth are so wet, so flashy. Sometimes when he talked, I could see a white Cert floating over his tongue, flicking in and out of sight like the smallest of buoys. I wanted him to save me. I wanted him to save me from myself. It occurred to me for the first time that summer that I might have had a difficult life before I met him. There was a rusted yellow truck in front of my house; inside, painfully yellow linoleum. His house across the highway was neat as a table setting. He had a magical symmetrical family: mother, father, sister, terrier. He had a baby grand piano, a square of wallpaper in a frame, and a living room whose whole fourth wall was a mirror. Facing the back of the house, you could see the front door with its diamond glass, and through it, the well-intentioned geometry of streets upon streets.

Instead of having sex, we built a catapult in the grass. What else could we do? We were barely fourteen. Childhood was almost all we'd ever known: every awkward pause brought us back to it. With relief, defeat, we sat on the driveway with the last Lego man in a Dixie cup. His face was just three dots—eye, eye, and mouth—and I remember thinking, what more, *what more* does anyone need? We launched three-dot man over the grass with wonderfully perfected, systematic, almost rote ambition. Over and over again. Childhood, by then, had been sucked dry by the unremitting soullessness of adolescence.

We met—how else?—in class. In April, Noah took out a pencil and set it on the floor beneath my desk. It lay like a hieroglyph or a scrap (which?) for me to decipher or retrieve. It was too deliberate to be addressed, and I felt stunned by my advantage. I'd practiced for this moment of superiority all my life. In a hundred mirrors, I had looked out from under my shelf of bangs and said: You could never understand me. But when the bell rang, he stood up as if no such thing as a pencil had ever existed—as if pencils were the stuff of nerdy fantasy novels, of speculative documentaries—and, bewildered, humiliated, I touched his sleeve. "Is that yours?"

This made him tuck in his pants, which were already tucked. I could see the misshapen wad of fabric beneath his belt that was the bottom part of his shirt. "No."

"Yes," I told him. My bangs were a roof, and I sat under them, waiting. I wanted him to admit that he was the one who laid the trap.

He held on tight to his backpack straps.

"You put it there," I said. "*You* dropped it."

"Want some lunch?" He took the pencil back. Like a good vampire living among humans, he acted as if he'd seen all this human work turn to wreckage before. He was patiently waiting it out, letting it crumble of its own accord.

At lunch I noticed his beautiful hands. Every time he lifted his sandwich, I could see his veins rise up and do a ghostly glide over his knuckles. By the end of the day, I knew he had a talent for math and a weird Charles Dickens brand of morality. He said to me, "Everything you think—it's true. So think well." I could hardly imagine what he meant by that. My mind felt like an intractable claw. Every thought was a secret wish to be better than other people. But Noah, I found out, had a well-organized heart. A mind full of unusual, ambitious thoughts, which he daily cultivated and tended. All spring we walked home from school together, discussing his theories. He wondered whether we could live without the moon—if, say, a meteor scraped it surgically, and without harming the earth, from the sky. Was it ornament or necessary? What were ornaments? What were necessities? What was surgery? What was harm?

"We've gotten used to the moon," I said, by way of conclusion. "We can't give it up." Every once in a while, this could happen. A certain combination of words achieved by accident could make me feel expansive, victorious. Luminous.

He said, "Do we even look at it? Do we even care?"

"I don't *need* to look at it. I've *decided*."

"Don't get mad at me," he said.

"I'm not mad," I told him, furious. In fact, I didn't care one way or the other about the moon. I just wanted to seem smart. But Noah could always make any victory of mine seem, at the last moment, unrelated to the real argument.

Our pattern was fixed when we got to his house. We each ate a bowl of cereal in silence, and then we went to his room where we took off our clothes, very careful not to mention or even affect to notice that this was what was happening. "Is this a new CD?" I'd ask. "Is that your sister's pen?" Once under the covers, we'd start discussing his theories again—ornaments versus necessities, a mooned versus a moonless world—and every time we touched it was as if by some extreme accident of circumstance. "Whoops!" Noah said once, as if he'd dropped a glass. A sprinkler blatted water against the window. There was a hand on my butt, a stuffed dog under my head, a face-shaped swirl of paint on the ceiling. Time crinkled up, got sticky. I can't remember what we talked about then. All I can remember is my arm going numb under the weight of his head, the leaking-sand sensation of blood leaving my fingers. I remember the click click of saliva breaking in his throat as he murmured in my ear. Then, after a while, Noah would get another idea—a bigger catapult, a tauter spring, a weapon we could build on wheels—and we'd dress in a rush, grateful to be done with the strained, shameful drudgery of coming up with things to say.

He wasn't a vampire, of course, but a Christian, a good one, so the third catapult we built was a raft. We just kept adding things and taking things off, until it was flat and huge and ready for water. Noah's parents weren't sure they approved of this, so before we tried it out they invited me to play Scrabble. They were white-haired and tall—looming people. Their white hair was incongruous with their faces, which were unlined and playful, almost girlish. They kept tickling each other as Noah distributed the wooden letters. Noah's little sister, Julie, arranged her pieces furtively under the coffee table. In my corner of the couch, I smoldered in the premature humiliation of defeat. I could feel my brain rising up in a slow, inevitable panic; before I knew it, the letters were too far away to be legible. I couldn't make out a word.

"Your turn," Noah's father said.

They watched me. It occurred to me then how bad my posture was, my spine a curled hook. I had a crop of pimples on my forehead and a long purple bruise on my arm from shoving my brother in a closet and forcing shut the door. I was still holding out hope that my body could go back to being what it was a year ago, which was effortless and completely forgettable, but that was starting to seem less and less likely. I tried to concentrate, but I didn't like how Noah's family was looking at me so long, hoping so hard that I was quiet and harmless and possibly Christian.

As they waited for me to finish my turn, Julie stood up and played a few bars of Bach on the baby grand piano. As she played with one hand, she leaned over to pet the dog with the other. "Dum, da-dum," she said.

"CERT," Noah's mother said to me, when I put my letters down. "Now, that's fine. Close enough, don't we think?" She looked around the room. "—to a real word."

Halfway through the game, Noah's father jumped up and said he had a book for me to borrow. He ran upstairs and bounded back down, setting the thing on my lap. He was a lawyer, Noah had said, but his firm had let him go a few months back, and he'd since been working on pending careers, spending a lot of time at the downtown library. "Just read the first page," he said. "Just read the first chapter."

"Here?" I asked.

"Just a few pages. There you go."

Now, sometimes, I think I can see the whole line of events that got me out of childhood—no event more or less important than the rest, just sequence, just time doing its march—but then, I was always on a precipice. I was always balking. For instance, when Noah's father said, "Go ahead, read it," I felt his kindness like a menace, and I considered refusing. Why be what they wanted? Why read what he said? But I knew as well as anyone how to *look* like I was good, so I took the book and smiled it down.

Later, after the ice cream had been served and after my dad had been called, Noah's father asked, "Did you make it to the end? What did you think?"

"It's interesting. That man in the desert—"

"He wasn't exactly a man."

"The angel in the desert—"

"Katie, do you believe in God?"

I refused to meet his hopeful gaze. Instead, I fixed my eyes on the abandoned Scrabble board with its rows and columns of letters, and it seemed sad to me then, almost pathetic, that so much time should be wasted on words that told no message and made no story. It was all just points.

"Sometimes, maybe," I said, because Noah's father was waiting for an answer and there wasn't any other way out. But I sliced my words down the middle into two equal pieces. The meaning said, "maybe," and the tone said this: "A nice person would fuck off, and you, I guess, are not a nice person."

The raft we built was wonderful, a great big flying saucer of plywood and two-by-fours, which we fastened together with screws and nails and set in the creek. It was high summer by then, and we knew we could float for miles before the creek hit the waterfall and fell, near Fort Snelling, into the Mississippi. We floated lazily through the suburban backyards of the city, startling children on their swing sets and fathers at their smoky grills. We used canoe paddles to get us through the rapids. Once, we were overtaken by a swarm of kayaks, sleek plastic boats that shot like bullets through the water. In our raft, we sat cross-legged on life-jackets, let the currents curl us around and around. We were happy. We got stuck in cattails and tree roots. When the creek widened out, we lay on our backs and let the sun, if it wanted, burn us. We were past sunscreen—we were way past all that. We floated feet-first under low hanging bridges, through golf-courses and under highways, past the penitentiary with its barbed-wire coils. The prisoners playing basketball were surprised to see us, and one of them rushed the fence and pretended to climb it, as if we could help row him an escape from jail. "No! Stay there!" Noah waved him down, laughing. "We'll come back! We'll come back for you later!"

Once, a red-winged blackbird dropped onto Noah's cap, balanced there for a moment, and then seemed to slide the air onto a nearby cattail.

Once, a boy on a skateboard raced us on the creek path to the next bridge, then spat a wad of gum onto my paddle. The gum clung to the wood like a grey, wrinkly leech. "Grow up!" Noah yelled at him, and the boy, who was maybe twelve, said, "I'm not the one on a shitty old board in the creek. *You* grow up!"

Late in the day, my dad showed up, waving at us as we floated under a bicycle path bridge near Lake Nokomis. He didn't say anything. He just stood with one hand in the air until we waved back, and then he set both hands on the railing and watched as we were sucked out of sight in the current under the bridge.

"What's he doing here?" Noah whispered as we ducked under the wood planks. "How'd he find us?"

"I don't know," I whispered back. "He's just looking after us, I guess. "

Overhead, my father was wheeling his three-speed bike across the bridge and back to the road. I could hear the low rumbling of the planks, the creaking adjustments and readjustments to his weight. I hoped he'd just go home. I knew he worried about me—I spent too much time on the roof, I watched too little TV—but I thought he seemed reassured now that I was spending so many of my days with Noah. A teenage girl with a boyfriend is, if nothing else, normal.

Noah lifted his paddle up and thudded it against a concrete piling. "He's looking after *you*, you mean."

"What's the difference?"

"He doesn't trust me. He thinks I'm making you into a Christian, or something."

I rolled my eyes. "He doesn't even *know* you're a Christian."

He paused, put his paddle on his lap. "Why not?"

"What do you mean, why not?"

When Noah was annoyed, he would smooth his voice down flat. No landmarks, no intonation. "You know what I mean. Are you embarrassed by it or something? You know what I mean."

Did I? Here again was the old temptation: the desire to prove something to him, to win, which would be the same as losing a different, more obscure argument. But I couldn't help myself. I did in fact know what he meant, or thought I did, and I wanted him to feel bad for speaking to me as if we weren't on the raft—as if we were still in his house, or else in his bed. I felt betrayed. "*It's* not important to me," I said, as the raft surged through the water and spit us out into the light. "I don't care about *that* at all. It's pretty insignificant to me, actually. I never think about it, that's why I didn't tell my dad. Who cares?"

After the raft sank and couldn't be repaired, we sat around for a few days with his sister at the park. Julie was a burgeoning athlete. She always had a tennis racket or a baseball bat, a muscle set that needed toning. Sometimes we could talk the neighborhood boys into letting her in a soccer game, and then we'd go back to Noah's empty house and draw up plans for our time machine. By July, Noah's bed was hot, a wrinkled coil of sheets that kept us turning from our bellies to our backs, from our backs to our bellies. We moved like stones in waves, like sunbathers. We didn't call it a time machine, of course. The title we put in the tab of our manila folder after we got dressed was: A Hypothesis for Quantum Tunneling. What I liked best was the library where we went after lunch because it was air-conditioned and mostly empty, just mothers with mottled babies in slings and sleeping homeless people. The books we read had been read by someone else, someone who folded the pages down and wrote in pencil little marginal notes, like, *The problem of the grandfather paradox.* "I don't know if this guy understood any of this," Noah said, excited. As he read, he scraped curled bits of wood from his pencil tip with a fingernail. "There's a whole fourth dimension you can't see with anything but math."

For Noah, this made the time machine so much better than the catapult or the raft. It was so much more inviolable and ambitious.

He forbade me from using the run-of-the-mill language of "moving" or "traveling" in time, and instead insisted on talking exclusively of worldlines and closed time-like curves, in which, Noah said, an event can be simultaneous with its cause, and may be able to cause itself. "This is something most people don't think about at *all*," Noah pointed out. It was hard for me to tell how serious Noah really was about this project. Sometimes it seemed as though we were mocking the people who believed this stuff, like the guy with the marginal note that said, *place - time = memory - mind.* ("How lame," Noah said. "How completely, unintentionally dumb.") And other times it seemed we were mocking them because they didn't believe it enough—weren't determined and talented enough to take it seriously.

One afternoon, I talked Noah into checking out our books from the library and walking to the 7-Eleven. We sat on the sidewalk outside, stabbing tunnels in red slush with our straws. "Can I have a sip of yours?" I asked. I wanted to put my mouth where Noah's mouth was, I wanted him to see my throat working.

But he was already standing up.

"I've got an idea," he said. "You want to hear what I'm thinking about?"

I didn't really. I was getting a little bored of relativity, and so I dawdled as we crossed the street, let a car get too close and honk at me. I gave the driver—a pregnant lady rubbing her belly—the finger.

Her expression was unruffled, almost smug, as if she expected this from me, as if I was just some punk teenager like all the others. Then I wanted to hold up my book on *General Relativity in the Age of Allegory* in my defense. I wanted to show her what her bullied, ordinary mind could not begin to comprehend. I wanted to make time twist into a miraculous disastrous tunnel and take its own tail in its mouth—*Ouroboros, Wormy Death Hole, Formula for Stasis, The Nourishment of God*—but the instant the words appeared, then disappeared, from my head, I tucked the book under my arm so she couldn't see it as she passed. "Come on," Noah called, but I was incensed at him, suddenly, and shouted back, "Did you even *look* for traffic before you stepped into the road? What the hell's *wrong* with you?"

He gave me a look like I'd kicked him. For the moment, though, I didn't care about hurting him.

The problem was it was getting harder for me to tell if I was far, far ahead of everyone else—or somehow behind other kids my age, the ones who spent their days at the pool and at Taco Bell.

I grew ashamed, a little secretive. One night, Ashley Leber from across the street called to ask if I could take over a baby-sitting job. After I agreed, she said she'd heard I built a boat with Noah and took it to the creek—"Noah's Ark," she called it. "Are you still dating that Evangelical freak?" she asked. "Excuse my language."

"No," I said. "Not really."

"Not that *you'd* be a freak for dating him. He's hot."

"Yeah," I said. "I guess."

I could barely remember liking those girls, Ashley and her friends, who lived on my block. Every day that summer, they rode their ten-speed bikes to the mall, where they ate samples of frozen yogurt from doll-sized spoons. "You can eat as much as you want," Ashley told me, "and it's all free, and you don't get fat."

I must have liked them once, however, because that summer they treated me with an evasive respect, like someone's frail grandma. Like someone who'd taken care of them once, and now was to be humored. It was true, I guess. When we were ten, when we were eleven, I'd taken care of them all. I'd ushered them one by one into the woods—though they were scared, though they were so often weepy and appalled—and I took their shoes from them, and I took their socks. I made their wimpy girl fantasies into categorical facts. I told them where to stand, how to walk, how to do the stories. *Look, the club-footed horse thief made you lame so you'd have to make love to him. Limp, limp. Look, the limping princess tried to escape on a horse stolen from the thief's stable. You, gallop. You, stop. Put your heart into it.* I didn't remember Ashley, in particular, being there with us. There were only believers and doubters: I saw no other distinctions, considered none of them friends. You either believed what the mind could do—and took your severed horse hoof and found what solace there was—or you didn't, and were a kid. I had no pity, no patience, for pretenders, for people who needed shoes or snacks. I converted them all. They loved me because I was the only one who could get them through it, past their own marginal, limited minds, which required so many little suicides, so much constant sacrifice, surrender after surrender.

Now, when Ashley rolled by on her bike, I could honestly say I didn't feel anything for her. She was nobody. A girl with a plastic hair-clip in her mouth, like a bit. She was someone else's pet. I didn't need her to stop her bike and ask me with such strained deference to come along, as if I ever needed anything from her. "There's a flavor with gum in it," she said, hesitating at my driveway.

"Okay," I said. But when she started a smile by pulling her hair by the roots into a ponytail, I added, "I've got stuff to do though. This project I'm working on."

She shrugged and made a lopsided ponytail with one hand. Rode on.

The project was going poorly, however. Noah's parents got worried that we were spending too much time alone, so they started calling him during the day when they were gone. By July they were taking turns, calling every hour, on the hour. His mother called from her desk at church and his father called from gas stations where he lunched on hotdogs. He was meeting contacts in the field, Noah said, looking for a job that let him be himself, which, I guess, meant not getting punished for speculating about angels. In the kitchen, Noah would wind the phone cord around his neck, like a noose, and politely reassure him. "Julie's at the neighbors. She's fine. I'm fine. The house keeps on not burning down."

More and more now, we stayed at the table with our books after cereal. Noah was getting impatient with our progress on a propulsion system for time dilation. He seemed harried by the numbers, stressed out. He didn't have time for taking the dog out, so I did that, and other chores too, like filling the dishwasher. At the table, Noah took notes on his father's legal pads, and when there was nothing else for me to do, I made doodles next to his notes. I drew rafts and vessels and boats, anything that could float away.

Once, the phone rang when Noah was in the middle of a troubling equation. He had his head in both hands, and I could see him squeezing his skull, the blue veins riding over his knuckles. His veins were like a second, more complicated hand that lived inside the ordinary one. He groaned. "Answer that, please? I'm working on something."

I stood up at once, feeling the complete uselessness of my limbs, which I could not arrange in a tidy, concentrated hunch over math the way Noah did. I was always crouching in my chair, pulling out a single strand of hair and setting it adrift in the sunshine with the dust.

"Well!" It was Noah's dad on the phone. He sounded startled, as if someone had come up from behind and said boo. "It's nice to get you on the phone, Katie. What are you up to today?"

"Not much."

"Okay. Well. Listen." He had nothing else to say, and in the wake of his last word I heard him change the phone to his other ear. I could actually hear his stubble scrape against the mouthpiece.

"Is there something I should tell Noah?"

"Tell him I'll be home at six?" He made it into a question. What he really wanted to know was something else, something only I could tell him.

But I felt no responsibility to reassure Noah's dad, who hadn't let me go home until I'd finished his book about a man who walked barefoot across the Sahara, who lay down and almost died of dehydration, and then got back up again when an angel arrived on a cloud. That man was a moron, a liar. His story wasn't convincing at all. "No problem!" I told Noah's dad now, egging him on a little because I knew I could. "I'll let Noah know. He's waiting for me, so I should get back to him. You won't be here for, what, like another five hours? No worries! We'll figure out *something* to do until Julie gets home."

The next day, Julie came home earlier than usual, and I put together a lunch for her that was three slices of cheese and a Popsicle on a plate. We went into the backyard so she could drip if she needed to. I noticed she had grass stains on her knees from a rough game of soccer and dried sweat under her ears. When she finished her Popsicle, she slid the whole stick in her mouth, like a knife eater, and then spat it hard across the yard. The dog took off after it.

"My dad said not to play at the park for more than an hour, which isn't long enough for a real game if anyone's any good." She looked at me suspiciously. "What are you and Noah doing with all those books, anyway? Studying for the SATs or something?"

She arched her body backwards into a bridge as she said this, and began to inch around—her head going red, her strawberry blond hair whisking the grass. For a moment, she reminded me of my girls in the woods, the best ones, who refused to give the excuse of their bodies. Those girls climbed two stories up a pine tree when I told them. They hung upside down from legs like hooks.

"It's not school work," I said. I didn't want her to think I was some kind of nerd, to confuse me with the kids who were always worrying about getting into a good college.

She pulled out of her bridge and lay flat in the grass. "Well, what?"

I decided to try the truth on her. She was back in her bridge before I said a word, and I thought, as she scuttled around with her shirt slipping over her head, she might understand. Her nipples faced me like eyes. "It's hard to explain," I sighed. "It's pretty complicated, but it's not about schoolwork. We don't care about college. We're working on something called a quantum tunnel." Julie sat down on the grass, hard, and because she didn't seem impressed at all, I added, "That's like a time machine."

"Noah's building a time machine?"

"And *I am*."

I could tell by her posture she was wary. She was afraid I wasn't taking her seriously, that I was mocking her because she was ten and I had nothing else to do with my time. She said, picking up a leaf and tearing it to bits, "Is that even possible?"

"Well, it seems, I guess, theoretically possible to travel," I wasn't supposed to use that word, "to *tunnel* into the future. But not the past. Nobody seems to agree about the past. But most everyone thinks you could go to the future."

"You're going to the future?" The way she said this—so slowly, a piece of leaf in her mouth—I could tell she was considering it now for real. I wanted very much, then, to crouch over and whisper in her ear, to convince her. Little girls are so pliable. It would be nothing, it would be like knocking over a full glass of water, to get her to believe me.

But then she bloomed back into her bridge and walked on her backwards-facing palms over to the driveway. "Aren't we going to the future already? What kind of time machine is that? What we already do."

She had a point, I guess, and I felt my fingers get stiff on my lap. Then I reminded myself: Julie never did have any real talent for making things up. "Well, the theory is it gets us there *faster* or something." I stood up. "Spit that leaf out of your mouth, okay? That's gross."

Noah began to give up hope in August. He'd been so sure we'd come to a conclusion one way or another by the end of the summer, but it seemed we were getting further and further away from a tenable theory rather than closer and closer. He kept trying to understand math that made him set his head on his book and groan, like a zombie. "We'll need a course in calculus," he moaned one afternoon. "We'll need to go to college, maybe graduate school. I kept thinking we could just skip over derivatives, but now I think we can't." He lifted his head and there was a welt on his cheek from where the book's staircase of pages had marked him.

We ate cereal and watched the dog pee under the deck because it was raining.

"Where's Julie?" Noah wondered, looking worried for once—as if she had just occurred to him for the first time all summer. We went and stood in the open threshold of the sliding glass door, where we could feel the displacement of air from the rain.

"I don't know," I said. "She's *your* sister."

Anything could wound him. Which was one of the reasons I loved him, I guess, and why I knew I would stick around for longer than made sense, maybe marry him. He sat down morosely on the planks of the stairs, let the rain drench him.

I said—sorry now for what I said, soothing him—"You're getting soaked. Come back inside."

"It doesn't matter."

"You look like a bad movie, seriously. There should be music so we can just sit and watch you and feel sad."

He started humming a song I didn't know, then stopped. "You know what?" He laughed in a way that didn't sound like laughing.

"My parents think we're *doing it*." He rubbed the rain off the face of his watch and gave it a heartbreaking look.

Right on cue, the phone started ringing. The very last word he said overlapped with the phone's first droning cry. Between each ring, the silence went on and on, and I was sure, each time, that that was the end. And then each time it rang again, long after I thought it had stopped.

"Doing it?" I laughed at his grammar. "What in the *world* makes you say that?"

He stood up. "Let's go inside. I don't want to talk about it."

Neither did I. We lay damply in his bed in silence. No small talk, for once, and no planning. At first I found the silence inordinately exciting. We lay naked on our backs without touching, and it occurred to me then that if he looked over at me, even once, he would see everything, everything. My knees felt welded together with sweat. Without any talk—without any urge to talk—to distract us, even my breathing felt enormous, wicked enough to disturb the bed as air went in and out of my chest. I breathed, and held my breath. Breathed.

But then I realized Noah was only silent because he was depressed. I felt his misery moving off him in immobilizing waves.

"Noah," I said. "We could build another raft. We could do something else."

"It's not that. I don't care if we build anything. I just want to know whether it's possible, you know? So we haven't wasted all this time on nothing. It doesn't have to *actually* happen."

The phone started up again, and between each ring, I waited.

But neither of us got out of bed.

After a moment, I took his hand and starting talking. I didn't know what I was talking about. I was telling stories, bullshitting, making things up, but mostly I was just hoping Noah would shift his shoulder into my breast and pretend it hadn't happened. I was hoping if I talked long enough about something else, we could pretend I wasn't taking his dick in my hand like an animal I'd caught by simply bending down and opening up my fingers.

There would be no time machine, of course, but we didn't say that.

I never told Noah about my girls in the woods, though I wish I had.

Emily Fridlund

They hung upside down from branches, and I watched their heads fill up, one by one, with blood. I stood on the ground and let them dangle. "I'm sick," some of them pleaded. "Let me come down." And I did. But the best ones stayed and were bats, were vampires. They crossed their wrists over their chests, and they didn't fall. They said they would fall, they said their legs were getting tired. They said there was a ringing in their ears (a music, I told them, a song for crisis), but they just kept on shining in the tree like Christmas decorations. Human flags. I didn't tell Noah, but if I had, I would have explained that they didn't fall, not one of them.

The strange thing about that woods when I think back on it is that it was just Mr. Ferter's untended backyard, with rolls of chicken wire beneath buckthorn and a bunch of rusty lawnmowers. I remember I had a stick that was twice as tall as I was. I hoisted it over my head, majestically I felt, and in this way I could touch those beet-red dangling hands (the ones who couldn't keep them crossed over their chests) and stir all that brackish hair. I could tap the bug-eyed nipples on their chests when they let their arms go and their shirts bunched up around their armpits. Even now I remember how good that felt. I felt everything as if the twigged point of the stick were my own fingertip, which was precise but so unwieldy as well—so tricky to manage. Nobody ever really appreciated that. The skill. The skill.

Just before school started, Noah's parents started making him go in twice a week for private talks with his minister. The first thing this minister did was forbid him to be alone in the house with his girlfriend. This wasn't much of an obstacle, though, because Noah could say with complete truthfulness that he and I had never even once discussed having that kind of relationship. Later, his minister revised his earlier recommendation and warned Noah not to spend time alone at home with a girl who did not share his moral values and his most sacred beliefs. "I told him we have lots of projects together, but he said I won't find peace." Noah looked hunched over and old when he told me. In keeping with the minister's rules, we were sitting in his driveway. "He said I will never be happy that way."

"Are you happy *now*?" We had the catapult out and had rigged up a system that smashed Lego man straight into the cement.

I shouldn't have asked it. The dog came out of the garden and scooped up Lego man with his mouth. Noah clapped his hands and ran after him. "*Leave* it!" he howled. He pried open the dog's face and wrenched Lego man free from its jaws. "*Bad* dog. Shame."

He came back, set a glistening Lego man in his Dixie cup, and I wondered then what it was like to be a real Christian, to live inside that box, to live with all those corners and walls—and way up at the top, just one little shuttered window.

"Noah," I said to him. "What would happen if we *could* go to the future, just skip over all this, and, ta da, be twenty-four or sixty-two?"

He was a child now. He was a boy throwing rocks at a dog. He didn't want to play this game. "*I* don't know."

I tried another tack. "Or what if you were, like, born without limbs. Without arms and without legs. Could you be content?"

"That doesn't make sense." But he sat down to think about it. He pulled the lever and sent Lego man skidding across cement on his chest. "Maybe. Maybe in certain circumstances."

"Or what if a meteor came and scraped Earth from the solar system? Whack. Would God be sad?"

"He would and he wouldn't. The earth is just an idea that God has, I think. A thought in His mind, which can't actually be—"

"Be?"

"I'm trying to think of the word. Changed. Damaged."

The dog skidded out from behind a bush, scooped up Lego man in his mouth, and ran off towards the creek. It was strange how satisfying that was, how glad I was to be done, finally, with the catapult game, and I told Noah in a rush that I was willing to believe the possibility that God existed.

He shook his head. "You *don't* believe in God."

"Sure I do," I said, as an experiment. I imagined the face I'd have to wear as a Christian, the knowing half-smile that you see in Jesus pictures, as if swallowing something dangerous without moving your lips. I thought, if I tried, I could learn to play the piano and be a generous but talented Scrabble player. I could have better posture. I'd convinced people of far stranger things. I had been one-legged, lame, a beetle, a murderer. I'd made children into bats.

He could have tested me. He could have pursued it so much further than that. But that was enough for him. "Come on," he said, standing up. "I'm hungry."

Inside we stirred cereal in cloudy milk and tossed the last soggy pieces to the dog. Then we lay the wrong way in Noah's bed, our heads hanging off one end and our feet hanging off the other. Over us, the people in the ceiling paint seemed unable to close their mouths; I could feel the ache that was the ache of their faces. Noah wanted to talk about time tables for the universe, but I had decided to act the good Christian—to be better, so much better than he was at this—and I wouldn't let him touch me, even by accident. We were naked, as usual, but I kept my body out of reach.

When he put his hand on my breast, I said, innocent as Adam's dust, "What are you doing, Noah?"

He barely blinked. He took his hand back and said, "Okay, here's the thing. I know it seems like a dead end, but I've been considering cosmological horizons as an important part of the Big Bang space time, which undermines our understanding of what can be observed in the past. As well as, I guess, our ability to influence future events."

"Stop that," I said, playing Good. I sounded uncertain, I thought, which was an acceptable way for a Good Christian to sound, given the circumstances.

He thumbed my nipple just once, so I said—as if sad, as if completely worn down—"Noah? Do you want to have sex?"

He was quiet for a moment. "*No*," he finally said. "All I'm trying to say is that—" He lifted his head up, took a breath, and when he spoke again he was whining. "I want to go back to what I was *saying*."

He put the backs of his hands over his eyes, dug his knuckles in. Our heads were still hanging off the bed, and I saw that his face had long ago filled with blood, a flush that made the veins in his forehead visible. Close as I was, I could see a dozen or more tiny lines, like cracks, all purple and branching scalp-ward.

That's when my plan changed slightly. That's when I saw that what we did and what we said were two different things, two sides of a wheel that went around and around and would never meet. So I took his dick in my hand and I squeezed it, gently, in rhythm with his words, which meant nothing. He seemed to like that. Then his words were the important part—he was describing the transparent nature of the universe after its opaque start—and what I did with my hand was completely insignificant, far too trivial for notice, something children did because they hadn't yet learned any better. "No, wait," he said once, but by then the wheel had gone around again and I wasn't listening to him anymore. I sat up, the world swinging to black as blood rushed to my head, and I climbed on top of him. I felt something like a stripe of pain painted down my gut, that's all. He jerked away once and gave in. He wouldn't look at me then, and I must have been crying because a strand of snot dangled from my nose. I leaned down over him to wipe it off. I meant to tell him when we were done with this, *listen, when we're done with this,* we could say whatever we wanted. We could say I was a Christian. We could say he was a virgin. We could go back to the past. But then the phone started ringing, and instead of saying this out loud, I crouched there over him, awkwardly, holding my dripping nose, waiting for the phone to stop.

~Checkmate~

Tara Mantel

Jeff Basco and I played chess all summer in the barn that smelled of manure and mold, sawdust and leather. We chewed on bits of sweetfeed and spit the naked oats on the concrete floor. We stared at the chess board, stringing games together back to back. We logged our gambits in our notebooks, in code, like spies. We set out bales of hay to stretch out on while we decided which moves to make. We examined each other's faces for hints. We ate bologna sandwiches with mayonnaise and drank Dr. Pepper.

This is what I shared with him. These were the hours I felt him live, when the backlight from the setting sun touched me, too, a flame at my toes, when the warmth moved up my legs and into my body like a spirit.

Jeff could have asked Mr. Kraus, the calculus teacher, to be reassigned, but he drove to my house every day to be with me, an inferior player, a young man of unremarkable intellect, a late-bloomer, quiet in the classroom, a fan of stars and lakeshores, and I believe he did this because he loved me.

I had not seen Jeff in the hallways before school let out, but there his name was on the sheet tacked to the bulletin board, paired with mine for summer chess practice. He was tall and thin and had a facial tic—he tightened the left side of his mouth, released it, then blinked both eyes hard, in an almost single action. On the right side of his neck, extending up to his lower jaw, was a large scar the color of an acorn.

We walked to the barn, where I had the bales spread out. "We can play here," I said. "It'll be quiet."

He dropped his backpack on the ground and pulled out a Thermos. I went to get the chess board, which I kept by the harnesses and saddles, and as I set up the game I watched him pour steaming liquid into the cup.

"I drink two cups of green tea every day," he said, "to improve my intuitive grasp of the game."

Later, he referred to a particular Karpov-Spassky game as a *superb specimen* that contained *traces of magnificence*.

He lived with his mother and sick grandfather in a big house near the center of town. He watched over his grandfather in the morning and early afternoon, and his mother took over when she got home from work.

"I don't know what's going to happen when school starts," Jeff said. "It was a rash decision to move here, but then, my mother is not known for her foresight." The side of his face tensed, his eyes blinked hard.

It took me only six moves to realize that Jeff was tournament material. He had an expert's repertoire and a veteran's intuition. I found out that he'd been playing since the seventh grade and by now was beating all the math teachers from the nearby high schools. He said that their games *lacked elegance*.

The tea came and went; I would listen as he peed in the crabgrass outside. I turned to look, once, saw the edges of the scar hook around the back of his neck. When he returned, I said, "How did it happen?"

"I fell into a fire, apparently," he said. "I have no memory of the incident."

As summer went on, I pieced together, but never could confirm, a fuller explanation: that his aunt had once dragged all their living room furniture to the center of the room and set fire to it, and that Jeff, a boy at the time, had wandered in at that moment from his nap, stumbled over a toy, and fell into the blaze.

Sometimes when I looked at him, I envisioned a child, hair on fire, a black spot on his neck where the flames bit. A kid who didn't wail, a kid numbed and tranquil with shock, a kid who never again lost his way in the night.

Sometimes I wanted to reach out, with burning palms, to touch that scar.

My love that summer was Mandy. I met her at a church retreat. She wore tight jeans and heavy eyeliner and had tiny freckles across her nose. Her voice cracked bewitchingly. She stole miniature bottles of booze from her dad's truck. She smoked marijuana. She had obscure origins and mysterious parents and sisters who were dropouts. She kept a flashlight in her purse.

At the retreat, we wanted to play a pop rendition of *Alleluia* on piano and acoustic guitar but never did. Instead, during the nights when we were supposed to be rehearsing, we sat out on the hill at the far back of the church lot, smoking and groping each other. I identified constellations for her: Ursa Major, Draco, and, using my binoculars, the M13 cluster in Hercules. She was actually interested. I watched her watch the stars. I watched the smeared white stripe in the sky, two sides of space sectioned down the middle.

Then her hand was on my chest, light and fluttery, her tongue in my ear, her cool fingers under my arms. Her touch became his touch, we were kids again, restless in sleeping bags scattered in bedrooms or living rooms. I lay closest to my cousin Phillip; I smelled his skin, felt the heat of his shoulder. He grew so still he moved in other ways I could only sense. He turned and placed his hand on my chest—an accident, a message. I sank into the earth, his elbow pushed into my ribcage. We grew up on hillsides and scrubby woodlands, we grew up on weekends, unsupervised.

I nudged Mandy. "It's midnight," I said.

"Past curfew," she said.

"I'll walk you back."

But we stayed on that hill, our hair and clothes pulling in the moist night, our faces washed out under the moon. She grabbed a magazine from her bag and used her flashlight to read me horoscopes.

"What sign are you?"

"Taurus."

"I'm Leo." She paused. "We're not a good match."

"I suppose we should stop talking to each other, then."

She turned a page of the magazine. "It says here that you should prepare for conflict with someone close to you, possibly a relative."

"I barely talk to my relatives."

She read more. "This is a good month for me for love."

"But not with me."

"Right."

I tore off a piece of the page, wanting to write her a note. But I couldn't think of what to write, so in the margins, I wrote gibberish, which started in my family as a car game. *Turd spankle writ large gangrenes to the left*, I wrote, and passed the paper to her.

She read it and snorted. "I don't get it, but it's funny." She took my pen and wrote something back. *Don't cookie-flutter my dangles.*

"Hey, that's pretty good," I said.

After the retreat, I pulled out the notes and dreamed about lying with Mandy in a sunny field. I forgot the sleeping bags and the dangerous cousin, and wrote the most sincere gibberish notes I could. Even gibberish poems. When Mandy came over, we'd go up in the loft of the barn, where I'd show them to her.

I gave her all of them, all of what I thought I was supposed to give. Nobody told me that my body spoke more languages than I possibly could.

Mr. Kraus called Jeff and me asking whether we wanted to participate in the chess tournament run out of the home of a local grandmaster. The winner would proceed to the next competition, and the winner of that to the next, all the way to state level. We'd have to practice hard.

A few days after the call, Mandy showed up unannounced. Jeff and I were in the barn, an hour into a game. When she came in, I introduced her to Jeff.

"Hi," he said. His eyes never left the board.

"It's his move," I said to Mandy, making a *shh* sign.

"Oh," she said, and sat down on a nearby bale of hay.

We played for ten minutes. Mandy said, "So, like, you guys play this every day?"

"Almost," I said.

She looked at the board. "Who's winning?"

Jeff rubbed his eyes.

"What?" she said.

"Nothing," I said. "It's just that you can't really tell sometimes who's winning. It's more about who's developing a better position."

Mandy got up, sat back down. She pushed back the cuticle of each fingernail. She dug around in her purse. She lit a cigarette, offered it to me, then Jeff, who fanned the smoke away with his hand.

"Whatever," she said.

Jeff's right knee began to bob up and down.

I moved my knight, then said, "Mandy, let's go up to the loft."

I led her up the ladder. She fell back on the bales. "What?"

"Shh," I said.

"He's weird," she said.

I lay down next to her, on my back. She threw a leg over me. I felt her breath on my neck. In my ear, she said, "We could fuck right now and he wouldn't even know."

"When he leaves we can do whatever we want."

She sat up. "Forget it. I'll just go."

"I'll call you later."

We climbed down the ladder. I watched her go to her car and pull away.

Jeff's eyes were on the board, his head cocked. "Knight to c1 was an excellent move," he said. "The more I look at it, the more I realize its depth."

Realize its depth.

I watched him for several minutes, let his focus and single-mindedness pull me in, down onto those sleeping bags, into that terrible scorched neck.

He said, "Tarrasch thought that chess consists of only three things: force, space, and time."

Sometimes I didn't even record my moves. I made it seem like I kept them all in my head, arranged in neat columns. Sometimes I just stopped and listened: a cat playing, rustling the straw in an open stall; the dull thud of hooves in the paddock; a mouse shooting along under the warped stall doors.

Sometimes I just watched his slender fingers sliding polished wood.

It was my cousin Phillip who proposed spying on the girls swimming in the quarry. He had been there many times before: he knew dates and times, which girls, how long. He knew when to leave the garage on our bikes and how to navigate the barely distinguishable path through the woods and where to put the bikes in case someone else had the same idea. He had his favorite girl, Samantha, and he knew all of the girls' names even though he didn't go to school with them. He knew how to climb the slope to get the best view, how to crawl forward and up without making any noise. He had a backpack, and there were binoculars inside, which he pulled out and adjusted. He had dirty magazines. He threw one to me and said, "That's what they're going to look like in three years."

I peered through the binoculars while propped up on my elbow, the way Phillip did. There were four girls out on the floating platform and two swimming out to them.

"Samantha's the one in the red suit," Phillip said.

Samantha and the other girls were rubbed down with oil, brown and slick as seals. I heard the two girls in the water call out to each other, but could not make out what they were saying.

"Let me see," Phillip said.

I handed him the binoculars and grabbed a magazine, which I paged through until I felt dizzy.

I looked at Phillip. *We could do anything right now and no one would know.*

"Oh, man, she's on her stomach now. Straps untied," Phillip said.

I stared up at his chin, his open mouth. *Take my hand again, put it on your chest. Remember?*

There was a commotion. I grabbed the binoculars. The girls had tied their suits and were jumping in the water one at a time, from the diving board. They were talking more now, and screaming.

Samantha was not the prettiest. "Who's in black?" I asked.

"Katie."

"Where do they live?"

Phillip took off his shirt. "I'm going to go out there."

"What?"

"Let's go, come on."

You can't. But he was gone—over the edge and down to the sand, to the waterline, where he stood momentarily before jumping in.

He must have talked to the girls, I don't know. I didn't look. I ran back to my bike and pedaled home.

What I meant was, *Don't go.*

Mandy was already at the park by the time Jeff and I got there. She was over by the monkey bars with some other girls, talking and turning the sand around with her foot. I couldn't get Jeff to leave the game for a day—he brought along a magnetic set, and during the car ride had arranged pieces and flashed the board at me, his face twisted up behind it. I was supposed to respond with the best series of plays given the configuration he set up. "Jeff, I'm driving," I said.

The tournament was coming up, which meant that Jeff wanted to practice more than ever. I watched him hunch over the chess board, notebook and pen propped on his knee, squinting against the evening sun angling in through the narrow windows in the loft walls or through cracks in the warped boards, watched him slap at the mosquitoes feeding on our ankles. In addition to his formal play and directed chess study with Mr. Kraus, he pursued secret chess projects—new twists on opening gambits, several personalized defenses.

Jeff and I walked across the wide shaded street to the park and found a spot under a large maple tree, which was located near the sand volleyball court. I spread out the blanket and set the cooler down.

"I'm going to find Mandy," I said.

Jeff propped himself against the tree. "She is a singular distraction," he said.

After a few volleyball games and a couple trips to the snack bar, I sat down next to Jeff, who was writing in his notebook. He put it down and flashed the magnetic board at me.

"The snack bar was out of green tea."

"Very funny."

"Wanna play volleyball?"

He looked at the court. "You want me to jump around hitting a ball over a net?"

"Yes, that's what I want."

"Maybe later."

Around dinnertime, the games broke up. Mandy had to babysit, so I offered to drive her home.

We loaded her things into my car. Jeff sat in the back seat, quiet. Mandy and I played twenty questions. Then I asked her what she wanted to do with her life. She said she wanted to be a florist, or else nothing. Maybe a teacher. But she wanted to work with younger kids, teach them every subject, so that she wouldn't get bored.

Jeff snorted.

When we got to Mandy's house I helped her carry her things to the porch. Then I got into the car and slammed the door.

I looked at him in the rearview mirror. "What's your problem?" I asked.

We could do anything right now.

"Mandy's friends were really hot," I said. "Don't you think?"

"No, they weren't," Jeff said. "Not to me, anyway."

"Come on."

"Did you ever stop to think that maybe Mandy likes you because she's easy?"

"No, she isn't."

"She doesn't even want to do anything with her life."

"No, she just doesn't want to play chess."

"She couldn't even if she tried."

I pulled out and turned onto the main road. We drove through town, past the new apartment buildings, then, farther on, past the abandoned drive-in theater.

"Okay, maybe not. So what? She's smarter than you think."

"You can do better."

I looked at him in the rearview mirror and gripped the steering wheel.

Jeff said, "I won't be able to come over for a few days. My grandpa's really sick."

Streetlights and shadow passed over him. I saw a one-story house on an open, rural road. I saw the bright and burning child, skin flaked and curled, eyelids singed, three stages before the final stage: brown, dimpled, permanent. I saw the living room floor with a hole in it; I saw how it was repaired but how the cinder stayed behind, lodged in the polish, merged into the fresh wall paint. How do you fall into a fire and live? The miracle of flesh: it grows back. From a gash in the neck to a new neck, from absence to substance.

Jeff said, "I have to make sure he's breathing."

I couldn't see Jeff bending over a bed, his ear to his grandfather's chest.

Don't go.

Mandy and I were driving along the bluffs when the sky turned a brownish-gold, then dark gray. We went to Dairy Queen and ordered cones. We had just gotten back into the car when the rain came down, so we parked and ate, raising our voices over the pounding of the drops on the car's roof, tasting ice cream off each other's tongues. By the time we pulled in my driveway, the sky had brightened.

We went around to the backyard and sat on the picnic table. Within minutes the top was too hot to touch. The humid air was hard to breathe, and left me winded. Mandy yanked off her shirt and re-tied her bathing suit straps. She passed me a folded piece of paper. "Naughty gibberish," she said. "For later."

I lay back on the seat of the picnic table. The heat traveled along my spine. In the distance I heard a shovel striking dirt, a man's voice calling out, the wind chimes from someone's porch.

We went to the barn and climbed up to the loft. From the window we could see the storm moving east—black clouds tumbling over themselves, blowing endlessly into counties, lakes. From her purse Mandy pulled out miniature bottles of brandy, gin, and vodka. She gave me the vodka and opened the brandy for herself. She threw her head back and guzzled. The contractions of her throat hypnotized me.

She lay down next to me, stretching out on her stomach, hiccuping softly, her hair falling on my forearm and giving me goose bumps. As she rolled onto her back, her hair dragged over the length of my arm, and a beam of sunlight washed over her. She raised the bottle to her mouth again.

I crawled over to her and kissed her stomach. She twisted and moaned. I reached down to unbutton her cutoffs.

She tugged at the waistline of my pants. "Let me ask you something," she said, and stopped. "I'm totally serious. Do you like guys?"

"What?"

"Guys. Do you like them?"

"No, I like you."

She said, "Would you ever do a girl and a guy at the same time?"

"I don't know."

She ran a finger along my belly. My stomach buckled. "No, you wouldn't," she said.

"Okay, so?"

"I think Jeff likes you. Do you ever notice that he never talks to me? Or to you, actually, when I'm around."

"I think he just really likes to play chess."

She is a singular distraction.

Not to me, anyway.

I turned on my back. For three summers, Phillip's trick was to jump fire on the sly. All the relatives sat around these small bonfires concocted in somebody's backyard on the Fourth of July or Labor Day weekend. It started as a dare, one cousin to another, to jump the firepit. The parents had gone inside—or almost inside, chatting on the steps of the back porch or finishing their beers in the driveway. We were overtired and hyped up on roasted marshmallows, and that's when someone would challenge someone else to eat a charred caterpillar or moon a passing car or jump over the fire.

Phillip was fourteen, athletic, coordinated, but his jump began too far back, and his foot slipped on some dry leaves, and when he landed he fell backward, which seemed to put his whole body into the flames, but as it was, only his left side caught the edge of the fire, and his shorts were smoking to prove it.

He shrugged it all off, but later, in the bathroom brushing our teeth, I smelled singed hair, saw the reddened arm, saw the shine of fresh burn above the waistband of his underwear.

Let me see it. I envisioned pink skin bubbled and blistered, felt the heat of his wound on my own skin.

In our sleeping bags, our feet were warmed on the calves of other legs as our child bodies twitched into sleep. The spaces between them let in cold drafts; as we slept we turned in to each other, closer—our dreams warmed our pillows, which were coated with evidence of deep sleep: loose hairs, tiny feathers, occasional specks of blood.

Our hips touched. I must have turned to him in the night, faced him with closed eyes. In the morning, the covers were disordered, some of them thrown off intentionally, some of them pulled away from another in the chilly stage of half-sleep. Our bodies had cooled, all of the night's suspicions carried off with the smell of pancakes and sausage as we kicked each other awake.

The tournament was on a Saturday. Jeff and I parked along the curb in front of a two-story house with lavender clapboard and light-blue awnings. Mr. Kraus, who had just arrived, parked across the street, then walked over to us. "You boys ready?" he asked.

He led us up the walkway and opened the front door, then led us through the kitchen and a hallway, then down a few steps into a damp, sunken living room, which had large windows all along the side of it, and which looked out onto a small fenced-in lot. On the walls were framed photos of famous matches, and the bookshelves on either side of the fireplace were stocked with matryoshka dolls, Civil War memorabilia, and chess books. On the piano, an old baby grand, were two antique chess sets—a turned wood and bone set, from France, and a Chinese ivory set with a silk-lined box.

Five boards had been set up on fold-out trays or card tables. Two had been placed on the dining room table.

A woman approached us. Mr. Kraus introduced her as Lilian. We all shook hands. She was thin and pale and had her hair pulled back in a low bun. She asked each of us to pick a number out of a hat. A few minutes later, she hushed the group and explained that we would play until eight o'clock, break for dinner, then play again until midnight. Any games that weren't finished by that time would continue the following night.

My number four matched a number four belonging to a woman in her thirties. Jeff sat at the dining room table and was also paired with a woman.

Eleven moves into my game, I captured my opponent's bishop but realized too late that doing so might leave my king side too exposed. Two moves later, her position outweighed my material advantage. When we broke for dinner, Jeff came over to examine the game.

"You got too complacent," he said. "Your weakness."

A couple weeks ago Jeff had loaned me all his strategy books—five-hundred-page behemoths. From them I knew that complacency in an aggressive midgame is a common pitfall.

"What about you?" I asked.

"Position, excellent; development, fantastic. Plus, Mr. Kraus told me she's known for her terrible endgame."

We regrouped. After two hours, my center fell apart and my own endgame virtually collapsed. My opponent didn't have to say checkmate.

I can't say I was disappointed, though Mr. Kraus might want to know how the game went. I'd tell him the truth: I played my best and lost.

I wandered over to the dining room table. Jeff's game seemd too quiet for him, his center not as secure as it could be, but he showed no sign of fatigue or frustration. I watched him shred the board with his eyes, watched his tic carry away his face in nearly consecutive spasms.

By midnight, the end was nowhere in sight.

During the ride home, Jeff was twitchy and excited. His postsession analysis told him that he was in an even better position than he thought.

He said, after a couple minutes, "So, what happened with you?"

"What?"

"You could have beat her."

"Maybe."

"Probably."

"I don't know," I said. "The game started out as one thing, but then became another." I cracked open a soda can. "I don't even feel like finding out why."

"You need a more effective philosophy," he said.

"I just do what seems right at the time. That's how I play."

The road got darker as we moved into the suburbs. Jeff said, "We'll go over some strategies tomorrow. Don't worry, we're in this together."

Mandy and I sat at the edge of the park's gravel parking lot eating sugary snow cones with plastic spoons. I couldn't take my eyes off the ice crystals and syrup melting on her tongue as she talked.

Mandy's father owned three Italian restaurants in the area, and today was the annual picnic for all the employees. The central feature of this park was a hill. It was more of a slope, really, but when I was younger the incline may as well have been that of a mountain. I'd trudge to the top and roll all the way down, the trees and flowers in the distance flickering in front of my eyes like the frames of an old filmstrip. When I finally rolled to a stop, my brain seemed to slide out of my ears.

Two sets of creaking bleachers bordered the softball field, where two teams now warmed up. Mandy and I sat along the first base line, picking crab grass and holding it between the outsides of our thumbs, blowing on it, trying to get it to whistle.

I had thought ahead enough to bring a blanket, so when Mandy nudged me and said, "Let's go to the hill," all we had to do was snag a few beers from the giant cooler located along the side wall of what were probably the skankiest bathrooms in all of the Midwest. She grabbed a few cans, wrapping them in my blanket. "Boss's daughter," she said. "Privileged status."

We walked to the side of the hill facing the pond. Eventually a bunch of younger kids came around, yelling to each other and gawking at us, so we ran down the hill to the opposite side of the pond. We looked at tadpoles and clumps of frog eggs, gelatinous clots anchored to a mass of underwater weeds. We were on the very edge of the water, and as she scanned the milkweed and cattails I stared at her feet squished in the muck, foamy aquatic curls circling her ankles. A long snarl of her hair trailed down, skimming the water's surface. I turned away from her slightly, to hide my erection.

Mandy said, "My friend thinks Jeff is cute. Should I call her? You could call Jeff."

"Nah," I said. "I mean, yeah, but let's do it some other time."

Two kids were drifting toward us. "Is it true that he has a messed-up family?" she asked.

"I don't know."

"It's totally okay with me if you like guys. My brother is gay."

"Seriously, I haven't really given this much thought. I don't think it's an issue."

"Maybe you're bi."

I rubbed my face. "Can we just change the subject? Please?"

She looked at me. "Whatever."

Two kids started splashing us. Mandy chased them for a few yards, then tripped and fell in the water. I ran to her and extended my arm to help her up, but she yanked on it, pulling me in. By the time I turned over and wiped my face she had straddled my body. Her eye makeup had smeared, and strands of hair were wrapped around her head and tangled in her earrings. We swam underneath a huge willow branch arching over the pond, and made out. As she sucked my neck I could smell her, salty and sulfuric.

I wanted to wrestle her to the ground, rip her top off, thread her hair through my fingers.

I came, quietly, in my pants.

It got dark, finally. We walked back to the field. The softball games were over. Mandy's dad loaded up vans with coolers and softball equipment, jangling his keys as he walked back and forth. The parking lot lights buzzed as winged night insects fluttered beneath them.

Jeff won the match and would proceed to the next level. I congratulated him when he came over to practice. "Though I can't understand how I'm helping you out," I said.

"You are essential to my progress," he said. "Which is more than I can say for my home situation."

Jeff sat in his car, the engine still running, the window halfway down. "My mom has to work longer hours all of a sudden." He squinted up at me. "I haven't had the proper atmosphere for serious practice."

"Maybe I can come over to practice with you," I said.

"My mom would never allow it," he said. "She's quite religious, but the 'sanctity of death' apparently means no one else gets to live. So to speak."

It was the most I had ever heard from him on the subject.

After he left I went out to the paddock and drained the raised water trough, which was permanently stationed against the barn wall and partially shaded by a giant clematis vine tangling its way up old chicken wire, and wiped it down, being careful to not give away too much of my presence to the family of swallows camped around the corner, under the roof's edge. I stuck the hose in the trough and turned on the spigot: in moments the scent of hot aluminum, rust, and riverbank.

No Jeff the next day. Or the next, or the next.

My mom was the one who told me that Jeff's grandfather had died, when the funeral was, and that Jeff would be gone by the end of summer.

"What do you feel like?" I asked. Mandy and I lay facing each other on the picnic table, resting our cheeks on the splintered wood.

"Play-Doh," she said. "What do you feel like?"

"A bag of sand."

"Sand fornicates ugly against wicked ramblings," she said.

"But can you wiggle medley after dark?"

"Only after snow cones die idiosyncratic."

"Die idiosyncratic," I repeated. "You have become an excellent speaker of gibberish."

I heard a car door. In moments, Jeff appeared around the side of the house. He looked down at me.

"I learned a really sweet variation and want to try it out," he said.

I sat up. "Are you okay?"

He blinked hard and followed it with a succession of lighter blinks. "Are we playing or what?"

"Um, I don't know. I suppose." I looked at Mandy and shrugged. "Just for a little while."

The barn was pleasantly cool. Mandy headed up to the loft with her headphones. We opened with the Spanish game, and now, five moves later, Jeff had just fixed a k-side pawn to strengthen his wing and, I suspected, to develop the bishop. I didn't detect a variation yet. "Are you going to be able to go to the next tournament game?" I asked.

"The future is uncertain."

"Where are you moving?"

"Probably back in with my dad, which won't work, and then I don't know."

A few minutes later, Mandy came down the ladder. "I have to use your bathroom," she said. She leaned in for a kiss and bumped the board with her knee. The pieces jumped and shifted, a few fell. "Oh, sorry," she said, and picked them up.

Jeff glared at her.

"Look," Mandy said to Jeff. "I'm sorry I ruined your stupid game. But you were only going to play for a little while anyway." She turned to me. "Eric, why don't we just get out of here."

"Well," Jeff said, checking his watch, "it has been forty-five minutes, an eternity, I know."

Mandy whirled around to face him. "Hey, asshole, why don't you just admit you want Eric."

Jeff laughed. "That's classic," he said.

"Hey, guys, let's do an experiment," Mandy said. "Let's watch while I give Jeff a big, sloppy kiss. What do you think, Jeff?"

Jeff froze. Mandy moved toward him but he jumped out of the chair before she could even touch him.

"Fag-got! Fag-got!" Mandy shouted, pumping her fist in the air.

Jeff, red-faced and shaking, kicked the chess board off the bales, and tore off.

Mandy laughed. "God, he so loves you."

"Fuck off," I said. "Everything was fine before you messed it up."

"Messed up what?"

"Go to hell. At least he's not in love with himself."

"What?"

"Why can't you just leave people alone?"

"Oh, I *so* will. Starting now."

At the funeral, I stood around nodding and smiling weakly. In the receiving line I said to Jeff, "Sorry about your grandfather," and moved on to the next person. I actually wanted to hear him drone on about Tarrasch, about how the queen acquired her mobility, about historic chess moments and trendy strategies. Mostly, though, I wanted to tell him that I didn't care about what Mandy said.

The next day, I drove to his house, ostensibly to return his chess set. I knocked on the door, but there was no answer. I left the box on the porch.

On moving day, late, I biked over but hung way back. The moving vans were gone, and the car, the only vehicle left, was packed to the brim. I got off my bike and watched Jeff and his mother lock up the house. They got in the car and backed out.

I wanted to wave as the car moved closer, but I froze. It pulled forward and turned out of sight.

The afternoon was quiet: nothing but the scratch of leaves blowing across the cement, a dog's bark, the hum of residential air conditioners. I pedaled away, grateful for the rush of wind in my ears.

I didn't see Mandy after that day in the barn. School started, and at times I almost forgot about her. During the last warm days of fall, I lazed around, mostly. I didn't open a single chess board. Instead, I took my favorite books up to the loft and read until dusk. Once, in the pale blue of the emerging moonlight, I peered over the ledge and saw a shadow out of the corner of my eye, heard the faintest of rustlings; but when I looked closer I saw nothing, and I knew that the sound was only that of a field mouse, maybe a toad, and that it had nothing at all to do with me.

~Ragpicker's Feast~

Pat Mayer

Light thinks it travels faster than anything but it's wrong. No matter how fast light travels, it finds the darkness has always got there first, and is waiting for it.
—Terry Pratchett

Her head was full of catalog dreams when she bumped across an Alabama potato field, hanging on the back of the truck like a tick on a dog. Her people had nothing except forked poles to prod crops out of other people's dirt, but the mail order notions were stuck in her brain like they'd been nailed there, and she wanted clothes that nobody else had already worn.

The leathery old potato farmer took a fancy to her. Migrant daughters fade fast, as though they carry a red cancelled stamp inside, but on that day, when she swam naked in the creek, she was as white and pink as an orchid's throat. She knew he was watching from the bushes so she turned and paddled on her back. That was all it took.

Her folks piled on the rusty truck, heading for work in the Georgia onion fields, but she stayed with the farmer. Every night he emptied his pockets onto the bedside table, and every morning the money was gone. She hid the coins and folding green in a coffee can in the barn. She could tolerate the farmer. She could tolerate anything. She suspected there must be something out there that she couldn't handle, but she hadn't come across it yet. Only the year before, her little brother had dropped a sickle in the field and took off two of his toes, staining the dirt with peripheral blood. She'd whipped off her own shirt and tied it around his foot. Later, she went back to the field and found the toes and buried them because every living thing deserves a decent burial.

After a few weeks, the farmer died. The sheriff wrote his report at the kitchen table while they rolled the farmer away under a sheet. She drifted alone in his empty rooms, trailing her fingers across furniture, wondering what would come next. The following day, she found out. The farmer's grown children drove up in a long black car, scattering chickens. They went into the house and grabbed her by her arms and threw her into the front yard. They tossed her catalog clothes after her. Silk and lace bought with potato money floated to the grass like wilted flowers. They yelled out the door and called her a gold digger and a whore. The oldest son cocked a shotgun. She snatched up what she could carry and ran down the road with silk slipping over her arms.

They had no idea what a dangerous thing they'd done. She hid all day where the willows bent over the creek and waited for them to leave. She watched the house lights blink off in the twilight. Car lights bumped down the road, first white, then red receding into the night. She sat by the creek in a damp breeze that carried cricket songs and waited. When the moon was straight overhead, she walked back to the house and got her money from the coffee can. She pulled cows and horses out of the barn and put them in a field, and got a box of long matches from the kitchen. The house and everything in it went up quick. The barn did, too. It was all built with old wood, rosin crystallized like amber in the seams of hard dry timbers and beams. She danced around the flames, throwing back a long shadow, her skin orange in fireglow, and then she slipped away, before the sheriff came back.

She spent the coffee can money on a one-room apartment over a two-car garage in town and worked nights at IHOP, always mail order broke. And that's all I know of my mother's early life. As for him, the man who fathered me, she knew only his name, but nothing else about him. He showed up at her apartment to cut off her water for non-payment, so she offered him a trade. He was tribal, full-blooded from the Reservation, with an appreciation for the barter system, so he took her up on it. He left the water hooked up but marked it disconnected and she fell off the books for five years. Even though he was brutal and sadistic, that trade was worth hundreds of dollars in free water, all for the cost of an afternoon of pain and dehumanization and a bit of crooked bookkeeping.

Mama hadn't paid the electric bill either. An anemic guy came to cut off her electricity and she made him the same offer, but he handed her a religious pamphlet instead. When he left, she had a copy of the Watchtower and no lights to read it by.

Nine months after her bargain with the sadistic water man, I was born. I had the dark look of my father, so I needed a name full of sunlight. She called me Sky. I'd been fathered by a cruel stranger, but I was a child, and to me, my mother's disparagement of my father was like a picture drawn on water. I thought he sounded romantic, a tool belt prince from a fairy tale, offering benevolent kisses and city utilities.

"Did you fall in love with him?" I asked.

She puckered her mouth like a drawstring and said, "I fell all right, on my hands and knees. I couldn't stand up after he beat me like a dog."

Our town is full of churches. We didn't have a house, but God had so many houses, one on every corner, bricks and steeples and wide front steps and double doors. I asked Mama how God could live in all the churches at once, and she said those places belonged to people, not God. God's name wasn't on the deed. She said it was better that I should learn about beauty. On Sundays we rode buses to museums to look at paintings of peaceful angels and babies with glowing halos, but sometimes the paintings showed saints at war and decapitated crusaders in battle. Mama said, "In art, good people have halos and bad people don't. In real life, you have to figure it out on your own."

At school, my teacher asked each of us, "What church do you go to?" She was writing on the blackboard with squeaky chalk, making a graph of all the denominations. The chalk made tapping sounds against the board. Outside, wind was blowing across the playground, clanging the chains of the swings. Chalk was tap-tapping, and then it was my turn. She swiveled to stare at me. There was chalk dust on the bosom of her dress. "Where do you go to church, Sky?"

"I go to church in museums."

"Museums? Why?"

"To look at pictures."

She was at a loss because I didn't fit her graph. There was no "museum" column. I'd ruined her project, even worse than those kids in the "none" column who didn't go to church. She looked at me as though I were a hair in her food. That night, I asked my mother, "Why did she look at me like that?"

Mama said, "She has a soul inside. She thinks it's sticky and sweet, like the jelly inside a doughnut, but it's not sweet. It's hard and cold, like a stone. Souls are nothing but stones inside people."

Even so, I didn't care. I wanted what other people had. "How can I get a soul?"

Mama answered, "A soul's not a hat, Sky. You can't buy one. You can't order a soul from a catalog. For people like us, there's no such thing as a soul. We're hollow inside. Can't you feel it? We're more like a chimney where fires burn."

And that's how it was to grow up with my mother.

Hollow.

When I graduated from high school, she said, "Sky, use what you have to get what you want, like I did at your age. You have something I didn't have, a heritage that's worth money. You should use it." So I went to college free on a Native American Grant because of my father. The college microchips were reluctant to give tribal offense. Offers came in the mail and I went two hundred miles to a college with lawns and trees and old buildings. I found out that the world was bigger than it had looked through all the windows of my past. Like a ragpicker at a feast, I was boggled by many choices.

I was paired with a Latino girl for a roommate as a cultural consideration by the anxious computer. Her name was Marisol and she was dark like me, with an exotic heritage like mine, but unlike me, she had a large family that cared for her. She had everything I wanted, but most of all she had a soul I could see behind her eyes.

I said, "I wish I had a soul like yours."

"We can pray for your soul," she said.

I said, "You'll have to teach me how to pray."

She said, "Catholic children learn to pray, to talk to God and Jesus and the Holy Mother. They learn to fast during Lent, they learn the art of charity, to be kind to others who are less fortunate."

I said, "That's me. Less fortunate."

She said, "I'll make you my project, to please the Holy Mother."

Her culture was rich in stories and parables. She taught me many tales. "I'm earning a soul, aren't I?" I asked, feeling full of stories, and much less hollow. "You're like the man who climbed to the top of a great building and jumped off," she answered. "As he fell, he said, 'So far, so good.' You won't understand the true meaning of what you've learned until something bad happens and you hit bottom. You must prove your devotion to God through suffering. It's too bad your religious training was so neglected."

"I was an accident of birth. My mother only wanted water, but she got me too."

I knelt beside Marisol every day. Her belief was strong, complete, mysterious, as unknown to me as the insides of the big brick churches back home. I was simply kneeling, earning a soul through cooperation. I was stealing piety. Marisol prayed and I listened, head bowed, forehead resting on my folded hands. I created a mantra: Prayer, Fasting, Charity. PrayerFastingCharity.

The forty days of Lent came and it was time for fasting. We gave up things we liked to eat and we ate fish on Fridays. Fasting wasn't difficult for me because I was a hollow girl, accustomed to emptiness. I went home to visit Mama during that time and she tried to feed me a hamburger. I told her I couldn't eat meat during Lent, and only fish on Friday. She said "Oh, you college kids and your fads."

For a reply, I told my mother one of Marisol's parables. "There were two kingdoms, one rich and one poor. The people of the poor kingdom were starving, so the ruler of the rich kingdom sent tons of seeds to them. He wanted them to grow crops and sustain themselves forever, but the people were so hungry, they ate the seeds."

"I don't get it," Mama said.

"Fasting teaches us patience and devotion. I'm earning a soul."

She shrugged. It was no use. She'd never understand because she lived with a hunger that would make her take what was in front of her. She would eat the seeds.

When I returned to school there was a new Catholic girl on campus, from Marisol's home town. They were friends. The new girl already knew how to be holy, so Marisol moved in with her and left me stunned and alone. She saw me as a lost cause, a hopeless shell, an impossible project. I pleaded, "Who'll show me how to earn a soul?"

She answered, "Four scholars paid a boatman to row them across a river. As he rowed, he told them he couldn't read nor write. The scholars told the boatman that he had wasted his life, he should've learned to read and write. When they were half way across, the boat capsized. The scholars were drowning, but the boatman began to swim to shore. When they called out to him for help, he told them they'd wasted their lives, they should've learned to swim."

I asked, "What's that suppose to mean?"

"It means you'll sink or swim on your own now."

She left and I sat on the edge of my bed for a long time. For the remainder of the semester, I lived alone. If Marisol saw me, she'd go the other way. I learned to walk with my eyes down, a soulless, empty girl. Then, I remembered my childhood spent in museums, the paintings of crusaders on pilgrimages to a strange and dusty Holy Land. I decided that I should journey to a strange and dusty land, as well. When I went home for the Christmas holidays, I applied to the Bureau of Indian Affairs and told them I was a student working on a cultural study and needed to interview a particular person. They gave me his last known address. I kept my plan to myself. I couldn't take the chance that my mother would stop me.

I found him in a clay-caked, rusted trailer on the Reservation. The barren site was strange and dusty indeed, and had a holy aura. So far so good. I parked my car on the packed dirt of his yard and balanced on the teetering cement blocks of his front step and knocked on the torn screen door. A cold wind blew across an empty field, stinging me with sand. He called for me to let myself in because he was too weak to get up. I stepped inside and saw him for the first time. He was sprawled in a sagging recliner and wore only old and shapeless pants. He was the color of leather. I was amazed by how old he looked, how thin and insubstantial. His long hair was greasy and streaked with gray. I told him I was his daughter. I stood over him in my big brown coat and reminded him that he'd had sex with my mother and then he'd beaten her like a dog. He said that wasn't possible, he'd never beat a dog. I described her and he shook his head and couldn't recall her. He was in the last stages of cirrhosis of the liver. Alcoholism, he confessed. My father, dark and bloated, was dying in front of an old television while a televangelist filled the screen with salvation in fuzzy pastels.

There was a squash blossom necklace around his neck, pure silver with turquoise and coral stones, a beautiful symbol of his stolen history. I stared at it and he told me he'd won it in a card game. He said he never took it off because it brought him luck. Yeah, bad luck, I said. He smiled and reached down to pet a bony hound that nestled in the litter next to his recliner. He told me to sit down and tell him about myself. As I talked, I realized that simply arriving at a destination was not charitable enough. I'd have to lie to my mother so that I could return here again and again, until it was over. I asked him, "Is there anything I can bring for you tomorrow?" He instantly took me for granted. "A bag of fried pork rinds and a six pack."

The next day, I stopped at a convenience store on the edge of the Reservation. The tub-bellied man behind the counter was a Reservation constable. I got pork rinds and beer, no I.D. required, and he counted my change and asked, "Where're you going?" I told him, and he said, "That sick guy? You went yesterday. I saw your car in the yard. You church?" He wiped his hands on his apron as though my presence had left a film.

I said, "Church? Yes, I'm on a mission."

"A missionary lady? You women always come here, but the rest of them aren't native, like you. You're one of us, aren't you? Listen, I know the guy's dying, so when it's over, don't call me. I can't leave the store. You church women handle the burial. Just let me know it happened and I'll do the paperwork." He pushed the paper bag toward me.

When I got to the trailer, my father popped the beers one by one and drank in huge professional swallows. He fed the pork rinds to the dog.

I returned to his trailer every day for a week. Cold winds blew powdery gray dirt under the door and the wall heater came on and off, the expanding metal coil clicking. Sometimes, he complained about the unbroken drought of winter and said he longed for rain. He said he wanted to hear rain one last time because he loved water, so I poured words over him. The dog slept at my feet while I sat on a sprung sofa and talked and talked. I told my father the parable of the man jumping from the building (so far so good), and the parable of the drowning scholars who should've learned to swim. He asked me what these strange stories meant and I said they were only stories. I told him they had no real meaning. He lacked the compassion to understand them and I couldn't summon the grace to explain their beauty to a dying stranger.

On Christmas day, the last day of his life, I told him the parable of two women who saw an object in the far, flat distance. One thought it was an eagle. The other said it was a wolf. When they approached, it flew away. The first woman said she'd been right, it was an eagle. The second woman said maybe not. Perhaps it'd been a wolf with wings. The parable made no sense to him, so I told him it meant that we see things as we choose to see them. For a few days, I saw him as my father, a wolf with wings.

That afternoon I sat quietly on the sofa while the man and the dog slept. I studied my father's grizzled face. His breathing slowed and slowed and finally stopped. There was nothing more. I'd never learned to be in his skin so I don't know if it was peaceful, I only know it was final. He'd moved across such a faint line, finer than silk. As for me, I told myself that he'd meant nothing and his death didn't matter because the purpose of the journey was to earn a soul and it was almost complete. There was one final task.

There are Catholic prayers for the dead, the Last Rites, but I never learned them. Marisol only said that people shouldn't die alone and someone must pray at the grave. I remembered my mother saying that every living thing deserves a decent burial. I didn't have a casket but that was no problem. Once a body is in the ground, nobody knows how it's encased. I had a dead body and a constable who couldn't leave the store. He had ordered me to handle it. Now it was all in my hands.

I felt fine, except for the silly way I was shaking and the confusion in my head, the breathlessness, a bit of nausea. I got in my car and drove deeper into the Reservation, following the power lines. The sky turned heavy, the color of wet cement. The long drought was ending and the air was about to break apart in the thunderheads blowing from the north, pushed by a cold wind. Prongs of lightning split the air and jumped down to the horizon in front of me, brilliant and crisp, followed by rolls of thunder. The air smelled like a hot iron skillet. The rain my father had wanted was finally going to fall.

I drove with my head down and my shoulders bent forward, my hands tight on the wheel and my face turned up, watching the power lines. I veered from the road when the wires branched off and followed them down a dirt drive to a small house in the middle of a fallow field. When I reached the house, a bunch of hounds in a pen kicked up a fuss, barking and snarling and scrapping with each other in the dirt, kicking up the dust and spraying spit while the thunder crashed. Sand and straw whipped up from the bare field in swirls as I climbed out of the car. I skirted the dog pen and knocked on the door with chapped knuckles, holding my coat together as the wind whipped my hair across my face.

Two tribal men, one young and one old, answered the knock. The old man peered curiously at me around the shoulder of the young man. There was a napkin tucked into the old man's collar because I'd interrupted their Christmas dinner. Warm air from the house smelled of cornbread, butter, baked turkey.

They were grandfather and grandson, full of polite tolerance for the unexpected Christmas visitor. Their posture was open and unafraid. I can only guess that they must've seen something in my face that made them take me seriously because they saw me not as a mere curiosity, but as an event to be experienced. The young man shook my hand. He said his name was Elmer and he explained that his grandfather was a Shaman, a holy man. The grandfather merely nodded and smiled and waited for me to explain why I was there. I told them what happened in the trailer and asked for their help to finish it. They said they'd known my father, and they'd help with the burial if it was okay with my church. I didn't tell them that the only church I'd ever known was simply a collection of parables in my head. They got into my car and rode back with me, three shovels in the trunk and no questions asked, as though this type of request came every day.

The three of us gouged out a shallow grave in the cracked clay beside my father's trailer as the wind pulled at our clothes. The sky was a mass of roiling thunderheads, gray on gray as we raced the oncoming rain. When the hole was done and the sides squared off, I asked Elmer and his grandfather to wait outside while I got the body ready. Breathing hard from the digging, I walked into the trailer and drew in the confined air that was like the smell that rises from an old empty drawer. My father was cold when I washed his face and wrapped him in a bed sheet. I took the squash blossom necklace from around his neck and dropped it into my coat pocket, and then I called the men inside. When we lifted him, he was just a hollow shell, not heavy at all.

We laid him on the ground beside the grave and the wind instantly peppered the sheet with sand. I said the Lord's Prayer I'd learned from Marisol but the gusts carried my self-conscious words away and the noise of my coat whipping against my legs was louder than my voice. The grandfather took over, invoking the Spirits of the Dead to guide my father into the afterlife. He was a perfect Shaman, every bit of him, as he lifted his hands above his head with his palms cupped and bounced on his knees like old worn springs and sang in his lovely, melancholy language. His long white hair trailed in the wind and his voice rose and fell with the assurance of his unshakable identity.

When the chant was over, we eased my father into the hole, and the past we'd never spent together slid in with him. The men told me to rest while they filled in the grave, grunting with the strain while I watched. Their shovels made sliding sounds and the clods of clay plopped on the sheet and against other clods, layer upon layer. Nobody spoke, and they finished just as the first big drops of rain thumped on the grave and soaked dark red circles into the mound of clay. The dog plopped on the dirt next to the mound and whimpered. A musty odor rose from his damp fur. I wiped my dirty hands against the sides of my coat and appealed to the old man for one more favor. He agreed to take the dog and asked me its name, but I didn't know. He said not to worry, the dog knew. I took the necklace from my pocket and gave it to him in gratitude. We hurried to my car while lightning twisted and crackled on the horizon.

I dropped them off at their home, men and dog, and drove back to my father's trailer. I went in and pushed a pile of old newspapers against the wall heater and they started to burn immediately. The smoke rose to form a wispy layer against the low ceiling as I hurried out, leaving the door open to fan the flames. I don't know why I caused a fire. Maybe I'd hit rock bottom, as Marisol predicted. I only know that the fire felt right, finished, and level. In those museum paintings of brave crusaders and pilgrims on their holy journeys, somewhere in the background, there were always cleansing flames licking against the remnants of ancient pillars.

I drove away from the strange landscape of the Reservation, a place so unworldly it was as though a chunk of the moon had fallen to earth and these quiet people had been exiled there to anchor it. It was an ancient place of secrets, acre after haunted acre, and my father's unmarked grave was another secret it would keep.

I traveled through the afternoon straight back to school, moving fast enough to outrun the storm. Holiday lights blinked cheerfully in the windows of homes along the roadsides. I could picture families inside, sharing their Christmas night supper and teasing, laughing, giving gifts. Sometimes the oncoming headlights became only a blur, two white stars bursting against my windshield until I lifted my fingers to my eyes to clear my vision and brought my wet hand back to the steering wheel.

That's when I knew I'd finally earned a soul.

It felt like a stone.

~See the Mississippi~

Dan Pope

The dog had been growling for nineteen hours, ever since we loaded him into the back seat of my '92 Chevette and wheeled out of the driveway of Ed's abandoned house in Cranston, Rhode Island, a thousand and some odd miles back along the interstate. Fiona and I were fleeing for a better life in the west, carrying with us the few possessions we wanted to retain, the luggage and boxes and furniture strapped to the roof and piled so high in the hatch-back that I could barely see out the rear-view mirror, especially when the dog stood on his front paws and blocked my view, glaring at me with his beady black eyes. "Move, Sheldon. Get out of the way, Sheldon," I would say, and the dog would growl in response. He had been growling his low and baleful growl, as I have said, ever since we began our trip, and nothing Fiona or I did made him cease — not dog biscuits (he'd gobbled an entire box, snarling quietly while he munched and chewed), not babytalk, not Mozart (his favorite, according to Fiona), not even slipping a half-sleeping pill under his tongue. He was a difficult dog to please. If I changed lanes or braked abruptly, he'd bark, and if I lowered the volume on the Mozart — God forbid — he'd pitch a fit and start howling like a wolf. He didn't look out the side windows, as dogs will do. Sheldon, rather, stared directly into the rear-view mirror, watching me as I drove, his eyes on mine. It was disconcerting, being under close, constant observation by a Dalmatian, particularly during the dark and windswept hours after midnight, while Fiona slept in the passenger's seat and I pushed onward, westward along Route 80, passing barren fields, darkened farmhouses, lonely silos, the buildings shuttered and battened, mile after forlorn mile. When the sun came up, somewhere in Illinois, the dog's growling began to sound decipherable to me — almost human-like expressions of pain and anguish — and by the time we reached the bridge that spanned the Mississippi River (the Fred Schwengel Memorial Bridge, according to the sign posted by the roadside), I couldn't stand the noise a moment longer, and I told Fiona so in those exact words.

She stretched and said, "Sheldon doesn't like cars."

"That's absurd. Dogs love riding in cars. They love watching the scenery and sticking their snouts out the window. All dogs love that."

"Not Sheldon," said Fiona. "He gets car sick."

"I don't care. I'm pulling over. I mean it this time."

Fiona yawned and looked out the passenger window. She said, "It's not as wide as I would have imagined."

It was mid-November, and the trees along the riverbanks were bare. Below, the river was black and fast-moving. You could see the ripples, the current rushing downstream. I had read about the Mississippi in history books and now I was passing over it, like so many rivers one crosses during a lifetime, and it seemed portentous to me because we were leaving the east behind along with the lives that we had botched back in Cranston, Rhode Island — mine, hers, Ed's — and yet it also seemed utterly commonplace: just another bridge, just another river, albeit a famous one, as rivers go.

I said, "Isn't everything?"

"What?"

"Different than you imagined it would be?"

She didn't answer, and I moved into the right-hand lane and took the next exit.

A half-mile down the river road we came to a small town that looked like a 1950s movie set; there was a Masonic temple, a funeral home, a steak house called Sneaky Pete's, a general store. *Birthplace of Buffalo Bill Cody*, read the banner stretched above the deserted main street.

She said, "I'm tired, Al. Let's check into a motel."

"I'm more tired than you. I haven't slept a wink with that damn dog growling."

"A motel, Al. Clean sheets. Cable TV. A hot bath. Wouldn't you like a hot bath, Al?"

I shook my head. "Motels don't take dogs. Besides, we can't afford it. We barely have enough money for gas."

I turned down a sloping side street, crossed the railroad tracks, and pulled into a small paved lot that edged against the riverbank. The Chevette rattled and coughed when I switched off the motor. Fiona and I looked through the bug-splattered windshield at the water. There were no other vehicles in the parking lot, and no people in sight. Sheldon straightened up and barked twice, loudly.

I said, "We've got to do something about the dog."

She said, "You know the thing I like best? Those little mints they leave on the pillow. They're waiting for you when you unlock the door. Wouldn't you like some mints, Al?"

"Let's stick to the subject, please."

"It's been a long time since we checked into a motel in the afternoon. How about we give it a go? What do you say to a giving it a go, Al? Wouldn't you like that?"

I was too tired to think about sex, and she was too. Her hair was bedraggled and her eyes were puffy slits, and we both smelled like b.o. We had been taking turns driving. She slept while I drove, and vice versa. We'd stopped only for gasoline, sundries, and rest-rooms. We figured if we proceeded in this fashion we'd reach Denver in approximately forty-eight hours total traveling time — maybe less. Then we'd unlock the door to her uncle's untenanted one-bedroom condo (water-damaged but rent-free) and celebrate our new place of residence with the bottle of champagne and steak tartare he'd promised to leave in the fridge. We'd breathe that fresh thin air and root for the Broncos. We'd have Thanksgiving turkey with Uncle Rudy and Aunt June and all their happy progeny whom we'd never met, a whole brood of friends and relations waiting to welcome us into their Coloradan lives.

That had been the plan, at least.

"Pass the pharmaceuticals," I said.

She removed the film canister from the glove compartment and handed it over. I flipped off the top. "Which are which?" I asked.

"Blue are speed, brown are sleeping pills," she informed me.

"Are you sure?"

"Of course I'm sure."

"What about the green ones?"

"What green ones?"

"These green ones."

She leaned over and looked down her nose into the canister. She'd bought the stuff from a mobster truck driver who frequented the Italian seafood joint on Federal Hill where she used to work. *All truckers have a stash*, she'd told me. *You just have to know how to ask.*

"Forget the green ones," she said. "Save the green ones for later."

I popped a blue, and Sheldon growled when he saw my Adam's Apple working the pill down my throat.

"He thinks you're eating something," said Fiona.

"Come, Sheldon," I said. I reached into the backseat, trying to gather the dog into my arms. "Good boy, Sheldon. What a good dog. Let's go. Here we go. Come on, boy. Upsy daisy."

Fiona said, "Where are you taking him?"

"See the Mississippi," I said.

The dog growled when I scooped him up, but not loudly. He was accustomed to being picked up because he suffered from hip dysplasia and couldn't walk anymore. He'd undergone acupuncture, osteopathy, electrostimulation, various medications — but nothing had stopped the progress of the disease. His back legs were stiff and unsteady; if he stood on all four legs for any longer than ten seconds, he'd fall down flat. Most people will put a dog to sleep when the animal can't walk anymore, but not Ed, my former best friend. Ed was a loyal master to that dog, or at least he was up until the day he found out about Fiona and me and lighted out for parts unknown. "Sheldon doesn't like thunderstorms, firecrackers or flashing lights," read the note he left behind. "Steak tartare gives him gas but otherwise he can eat almost anything. I've taken all the money. Ed."

Sometimes time passes when you're not paying attention. Maybe you've been staring at a river. The current flows downstream, the water laps against the bank. There is a smell of woodsmoke. A flag rustles in the wind. Geese pass overhead. After a while you blink. You scratch your head. You wonder, What time is it? What have I missed? How much time has gone by? A minute? An hour? A day? A year? Seven years?

Ed and I were firemen together. We worked three-day shifts, followed by three days off. You get to know someone pretty well when you spend twelve and a half hours a day together at the firehouse. We cooked, lifted weights, watched the Celtics, Bruins, Patriots and Red Sox, played gin rummy, ping pong, Scrabble and Parcheesi. We slept in bunks, snoring in rhythm. His presence was basic to me, like being alone.

I went with Ed the day he purchased Sheldon from a breeder in Warwick, Rhode Island. Dalmatian puppies all look pretty much the same. They have those black and white spots. How do you pick one and not another? What hand guides you? Chance? Will? Desire? Destiny? The puppy ran on his little wobbly legs directly to Ed and started licking his fingers through the fence of the pen. I said to Ed, "There's the one. That's your dog" and Ed said, "Sure looks like it, doesn't it? The little fella came right up to me." Later I would learn that picking out the first dog that comes to you out of a pack is the worst thing you can do, because that dog is the alpha male; he's been leading the pack, and he wants to lead you too. He'll make your life a living hell. But neither of us knew that, that day in Warwick, Rhode Island, seven years ago, when Ed gave the breeder five hundred dollars and took Sheldon home with him, and the very next day, or maybe it was a year later — I can't be certain anymore of time or dates because time started moving differently after I met her — Ed rescued Fiona from the balcony of a burning apartment building on college hill in Providence, Rhode Island (it was night; she was wearing a slip and nothing else; she was yelling, "I'm here, come get me!") and married her shortly thereafter, the next day, I think it was, or maybe it was a year later. Sheldon wore a black doggy-tuxedo. I was the best man.

What does one want out of life? For some people, this is a difficult question, but not me. A man like me doesn't want much. Primarily, he wants to be fed, fellated, and listened to. He wants to look into the eyes of a pretty woman and see adoration. He wants to share his innermost feelings without embarrassment. He wants to engage in frequent sexual congress with someone he cherishes because after twelve and a half hours at the firehouse he gets horny as a bastard. He wants someone he can trust not to engage in sexual congress with a third party while he is at the firehouse. He wants, in short, a wife and a dog to come home to. That's not asking much, but why was it so hard for me to find? Ed had found it. Why couldn't I?

Those days I was a searcher. I was always with someone different. Ed and Fiona would invite me to dinner and I'd go over to their house with Susan or Teresa or Michaela or Carla or Kathryn or Melissa or Melissa (there were two Melissas, one Irish, the other Filipino) and ring the doorbell and smile heartily and pat Sheldon on the top of the head and sit down to dinner and say things like, "This is great steak tartare, Ed. You'll have to give me the recipe sometime," and Ed would say, "Nothing to it, buddy. It's a cinch," and Fiona would sit across the table, tipping a glass of wine, smiling her mysterious smile while sizing up Susan or Teresa or Michaela or Carla or Kathryn or Melissa or Melissa.

"Thick calves," she would say the following day. Or: "A little broad in the behind, don't you think?" Or: "Does she always wear powder blue eye shadow?" Fiona's judgments were always indisputable, always decisive. From then onward I couldn't look at Susan or Teresa or Michaela or Carla or Kathryn or Melissa or Melissa without thinking about the thickness of her calves, the overabundance of powder blue eye shadow, the broadness of her behind, or any other trait Fiona had called to my attention. Ed did his best to stick up for my girlfriends. He'd say, "Don't listen to her, buddy. I thought she was pretty, if you don't mind me saying." He liked watching TV with the lights low, even on sunny afternoons. He'd close the shades and we'd sink into our respective couches in his dark den. We were big fans of the Boston teams. We watched every game — Red Sox in summer, Patriots in autumn, Celtics and Bruins in winter. Fiona would bring us snacks at halftime, filling the room with her scent. Sheldon would sit at my feet, and I'd slip him potato chips and peanuts, and when he wanted more he'd climb up next to me and lick my hand and whimper. I loved those afternoons at Ed and Fiona's. It felt like home to me, like family.

Imagine you're starving. All you can think about is food. You're ravenous with hunger. You're pleading for a bite to eat — a morsel, shoe leather, anything. Then someone puts dinner on the table in front of you — steak tartare, let's say. But you can't eat that steak tartare.

You're not allowed to eat that steak tartare because it's not your dinner. You didn't pay for it. It belongs to someone else. Your stomach is grumbling. You're dizzy with the aroma. The smell of the meat fills your nostrils, driving you mad. You believe you're losing your mind. After a while, a voice inside your head starts talking to the steak tartare. Hello, steak tartare. You sure look good tonight. I bet you taste good, don't you, steak tartare? I bet you want me to eat you. I bet you want me to sink my teeth into your flesh, don't you, steak tartare? I bet you'd like that, wouldn't you, steak tartare?

Actually that's not a very good analogy because it was her idea too, not mine alone. She had green eyes and red hair — red like those sunsets you see off Cape Cod, Massachusetts sometimes in August, when the beaches are empty and the boats are docked for the evening. She spoke with a British accent, called a truck a lorry, an elevator a lift and a jerk a wanker. I couldn't believe Ed's luck. I was a fireman, like Ed. I had labored long and hard, like Ed. We had worked side by side those many years. We had waited in the firehouse for the call to come, and when the call came he had kicked down the door and rescued Fiona from the burning balcony, and I had not. The rooms I entered were empty. I found only ash and debris. For seven years I kicked down doors and discovered nothing but the residue of flame. For seven years, I resisted. Then Fiona called me in the middle of the night and whispered the words I had always suspected were true. She said, "Do you ever get the feeling that you've made a mistake? That your life is a mistake? That something was supposed to happen, but didn't? That something, in fact, failed to happen? Do you ever get that feeling, Al? I do. I get that feeling all the time."

I should have told him then, at the start. He was my best friend; he was bound to figure it out. I should have taken him aside in the firehouse pantry away from our colleagues and said, "Ed, it's stronger than the both of us. Kill me. I don't care. I'd rather you kill me than invite me to dinner and make me sit at the table beside you and Fiona and Sheldon, like we have done on so many nights. She has red hair the color of fire, the color of a Cape Cod sunset. I am drawn to her, Ed, and she is drawn to me. In short, Ed, my dear friend, Ed, I'm in love with your wife." But I didn't say that. Instead, I took Fiona to the Super 8 motel in Scituate, Rhode Island and had motel sex with her while cars and trucks raced by on the highway outside our window.

I opened the car door and got out, carrying Sheldon.

Fiona rolled down her window. "There's a steak house up the road. I saw it on the way in. Maybe they serve tartare."

"I doubt it," I said. "That dish is a delicacy, and this is Iowa we're in now."

"It's raw meat, Al. Every restaurant has raw meat. What kind of delicacy is that?"

"French."

She sighed. "I'm tired and hungry. I want to go up to that steak house and get something to eat. I want to brush my teeth. I want to use the bathroom, for bloody Christ's sake. Let's forget about sightseeing for today, okay? Let's go get ourselves a big fat steak."

I shook my head, jostling Sheldon, and he growled and drooled spittle down my arm. "You see?" I said. "He just won't stop."

"You know something, Al. If I'd known it was going to be like this." She turned away, running a hand through her hair.

"Likewise," I said.

"Likewise what?"

"Likewise to whatever you were going to say."

Her eyes flashed. "You think you know what I'm going to say before I say it. You think you're some kind of mind reader?"

"Look, Fiona. We'll get your steak. After."

"What makes you think I'll be here, after?"

I ignored her, and carried Sheldon in my arms along the riverside. We passed the hulk of a double-decker riverboat, latched to the shore, the top deck sagging, the planking rotten. It appeared to be a sort of tourist attraction, condemned now to rot. Beyond the riverboat was the town green. There was a plaque commemorating war dead, two World War II howitzers aimed at the sky above the river, a gazebo, and a row of benches, positioned for river-watching. Each bench was inscribed with a placard bearing the name of a townsperson. I read the names aloud as we passed. "In memory of Philip Czachowski," I said.

"In memory of Robert Lenninger. In memory of Thomas Furlong. In memory of Sylvia Tolander. In memory of Ansgar Olsen. In memory of Ansgar Olsen. That's two for Ansgar Olsen. He must have been something special, I guess, to have two benches named after him, don't you think, Sheldon?"

We'd come to the edge of the green. I placed Sheldon on the grass beside the second Ansgar Olsen bench and took a seat beside him.

It was late afternoon. The sun splashed a pale pink and blue haze above the tree line on the opposite side of the river. The patterns of color seemed to melt together, and traces and trails of light slashed across the sky. I felt that I could grab the individual lines of light like you would grab a baton and wave it around.

"Look at the sunset," I said to Sheldon.

As I spoke, a cluster of birds came from the bare trees to our right — small black birds, hundreds of them. They flew in tight circles, around and around, in the shape of a whirlpool. They hovered in the sky above Sheldon and me. Then they started spiraling downward, until they were directly above my head, flapping their wings noisily. I was surprised how close they came and how small these birds were. I reached up to touch, but the birds lifted momentarily, away from my hand.

"Maybe they think we have breadcrumbs," I said.

Sheldon didn't seem concerned about the birds. He was busily sniffing the grass, his snout pointed toward the river. I watched the water, and the riverbank seemed to be swaying, rocking with the current, and I felt I had to sit down, and then I realized I was sitting down and that I should instead get up and go, that it was time to leave. I rose from the bench, as quietly as I could, and took a few steps toward the parking lot. The birds moved with me, hovering over my head.

"Where do you think you're going?"

I stopped and turned around. There was no one in sight, only my '92 Chevette, parked in the distance.

"Well?"

I said, "Sheldon?"

"What?"

"You can talk?"

"Yeah."

"I can't believe it. When did you learn to talk?"

"I always knew how."

The dog seemed to be giving off a halo of light. His white and black spots moved and melted together, forming and reforming patterns that suggested some meaning just beyond my comprehension.

I said, "I think there was something in that pill."

Sheldon's voice had a mechanical quality, like a person who had suffered a tracheotomy and spoke out of a box in his neck. He said, "I'm hungry. Get me something to eat."

"I can't, Sheldon. I have to go."

"You think you can just leave me here and go away? Fat chance."

"I'm sorry."

"Ed wouldn't like this. Not one bit. Wait until he finds out."

"Ed's gone. He took all my money and left. He got me fired from my job. He left you alone, Sheldon."

"You fucked his wife."

The flapping of the wings grew louder. I waved my hand above my head, trying to scare the birds off. I felt the soft underside of one's wing, the briefest of touches.

"Now you're stuck with her, and you don't even like her very much. You idiot. Look what you've gotten yourself into."

I turned and started walking away, and Sheldon raised himself on all fours and took a few wobbly steps toward me and barked four times, loudly. Then his legs gave out and he collapsed on the grass. He said, "I'd bite you if I could. I should've bitten you when I had the chance."

"I'm sorry, Sheldon. Someone will come along. They'll give you something to eat. It's nice here. You'll like it here. They're nice people, I bet. Look at all the benches. People come here to sit and watch the river."

"Nah," he said.

"Really. You'll be better off."

He raised his snout and sniffed the air. He said in his mechanical voice, "There's something dead in those trees there. A possum, or something. Maybe a porcupine. Let's go down and see. Carry me."

"I can't, Sheldon. Fiona's waiting."

"I can smell lots of stuff. This time of day, the wind carries the scent of everything that people are cooking inside their homes. It makes me hungry. I'm hungry all the time. You never gave me enough to eat. Ed fed me a lot better."

I turned and headed back to the car, and the birds followed, swarming and circling above my head, and when I opened the door to my '92 Chevette they flew inside with me, hundreds of small black birds, flapping their wings. It would take a long time, I figured, for Fiona and me to clear them out and get back on our way.

~House of Guns~

Mary Helen Specht

Justin hadn't planned on coming back to Texas for Christmas. He only flew home from Boston, where he was attending graduate school, because his mother was stirring things up again. Threatening to put his grandmother into a Home. Threatening ridiculousness.

His grandmother had just turned seventy. She lived in the guesthouse—he called it the House of Guns—with its wraparound porch from which, on one side, you could see the corral and the hayfield and, from the other, the entrance to the main ranch house twenty yards away, which was post-and-beam and looked like an enormous log cabin. In a reversal of the houses' given names, Justin and his grandmother were the only ones sleeping in the guesthouse, while all the actual guests were staying in the main house with Justin's mother and her new husband Paul.

Justin sat on the hayfield-facing porch in one of the seven rocking chairs lined up in a row, smoking a cigarette and waiting for his grandmother. The wrist of his smoking hand was wrapped in the multi-colored rubber bands he used to secure his architectural drawings into rolls. Slumped with his legs crossed and his cigarette pinched between two fingers, Justin was going for the look of listless entitlement. He had high cheekbones his mother called imperial.

When his grandmother finally appeared, she was wearing red silk pajamas and a ratty ankle-length fur in honor of Christmas dinner. She yelled at him, unprovoked, "When you get to be my age you can wear whatever the hell you like." But she was not angry. She sat down beside him and ran her fingers through the matted fur of her coat—a wolf with mange. It was becoming hard for him to remember a time when she hadn't been like this—years ago—when she hadn't been going crazy. Justin tried to see the Hole through the back of his grandmother's head. Was it beneath one of the springy white curls, he wondered? Was it much bigger than the Hole in his own head?

"In the newspaper, the mayor called for all city fountains to be turned on. Real pretty. They're real pretty."

"What fountains? Where?" he asked, taking her papery hand between his own and looking across the pasture as if he might find marble spigots sprouting from the Frog Pond. This was how conversation went with his grandmother, who spoke with her head tilted, clip-on pearl earrings weighing down her thin, leaf-like earlobes.

"Not here, boy. In Boston. Where I live," she said, as if she were always having to repeat herself.

"What do you do there?"

"I go to Haymarket for the clams, and I squeeze hot sauce and a quarter of a lemon on each one, and they are still briny, having only just been snatched from the sea."

She was quoting from the letters he'd sent from graduate school, adding a bit of herself here and there until he could no longer remember how it really went. When he'd lived here at the ranch in high school, they did this all the time. They sat on this porch, and she told pieces of stories, things all mixed up, her life and her husband's and her children's all running together, swirling like a snail shell into one continuous spiral. Now it was usually his life that became the stuffing to make up her own.

Once she'd told him, and he wasn't sure where she got it, that the worst part of growing older was this: people passed away until there wasn't anyone left to be proud of you. She was dying, and he was starting to understand what she meant.

"My next assignment is to design something for underground," he said, flicking his cigarette onto the gravel surrounding the porch like a mote, turning his gold-flecked eyes on his grandmother. "I've drawn spaces in the shape of large cylinders, like grain silos turned on their sides, and there will be a strip of glass running along each one at the top, at the ground surface. Above: tulips everywhere."

"Underground the tunnels make your mucus black with steel dust, and bits of mica surround you like false stars. There are a dozen men in a row swinging sledgehammers in discord with one another, and the sparks run red to yellow," she said, and Justin was amazed she hadn't missed a beat. She'd forgotten so much, but not any of this.

Her tendency to quote from letters, letters she'd revised and improved on over the years, made her sound like a bad television actor whose lines were too perfect, too flatly delivered to be real. The allusion to the tunnels came from a man she'd fallen for before marrying his grandfather, during a trip she'd made to New York City with her family. The lover was a subway track worker who wrote her letters for years until one day he didn't. His grandmother wouldn't respond if asked directly about the past; she didn't see it that way anymore, as a series of events that had happened to her. She could only find it indirectly, by association.

She suddenly remembered her glasses, told him she was blind as a bat without her glasses, could he please go fetch them. He left her rocking on the porch and walked inside the guesthouse, straightening the corduroy jacket it had been too cold to wear in Boston, and found them perched on the nightstand in her room. They were vanity glasses from the fifties, black with white rhinestones; his grandmother could see perfectly fine.

He retraced his steps, down the narrow hallway and back into the living room with its limestone fireplace and various taxidermied animal trophies. While the main house dated from the early 1800s, the guesthouse had only been added after his grandfather bought the ranch in 1938. On Justin's right, as he headed for the door to the porch, was a bookshelf built into and covering an entire wall. A section of it, however, was actually a camouflaged door that opened onto a tiny room filled with rifles and pistols lined up like infantry—it was the reason he called the guesthouse the House of Guns.

As a child, he wasn't allowed inside, although he knew it was there because the hallway was longer than it should have been, and so he'd imagined a place with books of spells and beakers and wide-eyed animals suspended in jars. When college applications asked for an essay about a personal rite of passage, he'd written about the time his grandfather first showed him what was actually inside the hidden room. He was twelve and finally old enough to be taken along on hunting trips. His grandfather, lean muscled with thick white hair, had held onto his shoulders, smiling proudly as Justin stared gaping at the room. But it wasn't the guns, although Justin did eventually become a proficient hunter, it was the place itself, its mystery made manifest. That was when he first became interested in buildings and the secrets they held within them. And later Brutalism: A style inspired by High Modernist architecture that, when he found it, he recognized as the embodiment of his entire life thus far. The Robin Hood Gardens, an enormous East London housing complex with aerial walkways encased in long slab blocks. La Tourette Monastery in Lyons with its concrete stilts, undulating thick and thin, supporting an upper-story covered with tiny grid-like windows that cantilevers over a grassy slope. Buildings that were incongruous, that mirrored their guts externally, that were stronger than you were and made you feel every corner and contour as they butted up hard against space, against flesh, willing you to press your body flat along their blank slates of steel and poured concrete and glass.

Justin let the screen door of the guesthouse slam behind him and handed his grandmother her glasses. Time to go to the main house, he told her. She stepped regally onto the stone path, a Carousel pony in bedroom slippers, and they walked holding hands, fingers entwining like new lovers.

It had been almost a year since Justin found out that latent within his own brain was the same disease destroying his grandmother. He ate fish practically every day and drank large glasses of Pomegranate juice, but the doctors said it was still there, tangling and complicating itself with more neurotendrils, a word he invented that made him think of the ivy blotting out the windows of the buildings back at Harvard. Maybe he should stop drinking, they said. And smoking cigarettes. He was twenty-six and did not consider these steps necessary. After all, his grandmother might be crazy, but, watching her in the silk pajamas and fur, he thought, at least she hasn't lost her sense of fashion.

Justin had been diagnosed with what he called the Hole at Mass General after several non-alcohol-induced blackouts. After receiving the results from the CT scan, the one that confirmed what the doctors already suspected, Justin went to a bar, drank a bottle of wine, and tried to drive somewhere, anywhere. He wasn't hammered, but still he pulled out of the parallel parking space and smashed directly into the front bumper of a car. Standing on the edge of a children's plastic playground, Justin handed his driver's license and insurance to the stranger named Abdul and began to sob. As he did so, Abdul became uncomfortable, repeating, Don't cry, Mister. It is done. And Justin later thought to himself: but that's what all grief is—sorrow for what we can't change.

The Hole did not strike suddenly, was not an instant killer; his grandmother had in fact lived to be an old woman. The Hole usually came on slowly: it stamped out the mind first and, through the mind, the body. But "stamped out" was probably the wrong phrase; it changed the mind, uprooting it and planting it into a new pattern, like crop circles that could only be deciphered from above. One couldn't predict the part of the brain it would affect first, but once it arrived at the brain stem, destroying critical functions of breathing and digestion, the end was swift. In his grandmother, it had mostly transformed her memory and cognitive function—as well as freakishly improving her vision—but she was now beginning to lose muscle control. His family was one of twenty in North America to have been diagnosed with this particular Hole. They were lucky that way.

As they reached the main house, his grandmother threw open the screen door and practically screamed, "I am dying. I am starving to fucking death here."

"I got a letter from that old girlfriend of yours," his mother said, ignoring her, not turning from the counter where she was glazing sweet potatoes. "The one who used to be in that band with you." The walls of the kitchen were covered with retro-style posters of 1950s canned goods: Strickley's green beans and Campbell's tomato soup.

"Christ, Mom. We were never in a band together," he said, sitting astride a turquoise-painted chair, forearms draped across the chair back.

"But that's what she always says."

"Yeah, well, she talks a mean band," he said, watching his grandmother gnaw on the flesh of a Kalamata olive and spit the seed into the pot of garlic mashed potatoes heating on the old stove with its bleach-white edges rounded like a spaceship. Justin smiled at her. "We went out a few times, that's all." He felt no need to admit anything more.

"That doesn't mean you weren't in a band together," replied his mother, tying her bottle-blond hair up into a handkerchief.

"As usual, you don't know what you're talking about," he said. The girl under discussion, now a woman who sold plants in Far West Texas, was Valerie Valentine. She had lived on a neighboring ranch and the two of them used to drive to a fruit stand outside of Pecos and buy melons that made their fingers and mouths so sticky they were forced to lick each other clean. If they'd married, he wouldn't have let her change her name, maybe even would have taken it, but she eventually left him for a man who wore baby blue v-neck sweaters. He had no idea where Val got this band shit.

"She's still not married, you know."

"Don't even," he said, his voice suddenly low. "Do you think I'm that stupid?" Justin told his mother she couldn't manipulate him, that he wasn't going to drop out of school and move back to the ranch just because she dangled an available ex-screw in front of his face. He'd been gearing up for this confrontation ever since the phone call he received two weeks earlier at his Cambridge apartment; the conversation had boiled down to this: his mother said she could no longer handle being the sole caretaker of his grandmother, it had become too much. The phrase nursing home was tossed like a grenade.

"I don't care what you decide. But I'm not doing this alone anymore," she said, continuing to stir-fry the green beans, tossing them lightly in the pan, her voice steady, as if she were discussing the gravy. Ever since he was diagnosed with the Hole, his mother had absorbed Justin's anger, his outbursts, without flinching or shifting expression, as if they were something to be endured rather than answered. "It's like I'm a little girl all over again, being yelled at by her for everything, only this time around she really is nuts." His mother's face was red and splotchy from the stovetop heat, and Justin did feel bad for her. But he felt worse for himself and for his grandmother and for how much of life was out of his control. The Hole had skipped his mother, like a stone skimming along the surface of the pond, and so what did she know about anything?

"Alone? What about Paul? Doesn't he help you?" he asked, propping his chin on his forearms, feeling the lines of the corduroy on his neck. His mother's new husband had recently moved out to live with her at the ranch. She told Justin his grandmother was not Paul's responsibility, and when he said, "And she is mine?" his mother answered: that was up to him.

"Help or Home. That's what it comes down to," she said. "You will come back to help me or I'll find a place that will."

Justin retreated to what he referred to as the Vomit Bathroom, not because he'd ever vomited there, although it was possible, but because it was brimming with sheaths of lace and hokey sayings embroidered in pink—No Thieving or Loose Women—and country kitsch: wooden cows and miniature butter churners and crap like that. Sitting on the edge of the claw-foot tub, his thin frame crumpled. He knew he was acting like a child, that he should be out there helping prepare dinner, but the argument aside, this domestic side of his mother that only emerged around holidays disturbed him. Because while this was where he stayed when he came home to Texas, his childhood had been spent in Houston eating Chinese take-out in a brick bungalow filled with the detritus of his mother's projects: heaps of antique doorknobs, jagged pieces of stained glass, chicken wire left over from the sculpture of an anatomically correct male angel. Back then he had also been one of his mother's projects. But ever since they'd moved here to Fayetteville County, there'd been a distance between them, maybe from the strain of nursing her own mother or maybe not. Maybe it was just what happened when a son grew up.

They had moved out here when he was in high school, after his grandfather died, to take care of his already deteriorating grandmother. Justin had refused to attend school in the middle of nowhere; he finished his last year by taking correspondence classes through the mail. He got used to being pretty much alone, just him and his grandmother rocking back and forth in the chairs on the porch of the House of Guns. On the weekends sometimes, Valerie Valentine rode her father's tractor over to see him, floral skirts flapping around her knees, and they would lie in the fields and talk about turning the ranch into an artist colony, about letting the cows wander wherever they wanted, into the houses and barns, saving them from slaughter. These days, however, that was exactly the part of ranching he liked to watch—the butchery; he was becoming accustomed to the idea of death.

From inside the Vomit Bathroom, Justin heard the rest of the Christmas guests return, boots stomping and voices shrill, from the tour Paul had been conducting of the little vineyard and the watering tank and Krebb's cemetery across the Farm-to-Market road. He might even have driven them to the general store, which sold everything from condoms to beef jerky while also serving as post office and polling place. He would tell them that back when the Democrats ruled the rural vote, in the primaries Republicans had to vote outside the store, out back with the manure. It was obvious to Justin that Paul enjoyed playing host; he shuttled people back and forth, made dramatic displays, filled up the room with his gregariousness. He felt right at home.

His mother had been too busy preparing bedrooms and food to pick Justin up from the airport in Houston when he'd arrived the day before—"and it's not as if I can leave your grandmother home alone"— and so Paul came in Justin's mother's faded blue pickup and honked the horn once without getting out.

The two of them were silent most of the drive until they turned off the Interstate and Paul asked if Justin wanted to use the barn for studio space while he was home. "I've got it set up as my woodworking shop right now, but I'll be too busy the next coupla' few weeks to get anything done out there. It's all yours if you want it."

Back when Paul began dating his mother, he was always giving Justin things: a 35mm camera, a cell phone. But what pissed Justin off, besides the flagrant brown nosing, was that Paul's gifts were all leftovers, hand-me-downs. He would buy himself a new camera and give Justin his old one: Congratulations on your acceptance to Harvard! Here's an old gadget I don't need anymore! And now, thought Justin, Paul was trying to offer him space in his own family's barn? Unbelievable. "That barn is haunted," he said.

"So I've heard," Paul replied. "You don't actually believe that bull honky?"

"It has nothing to with what I believe," Justin said cryptically, his

Mary Helen Specht

hand pressed against the dashboard to steady him as they flew down the unpaved road, "It has to do with the way things are."

This year they had a full house for Christmas. His mother's only brother, Uncle Charlie, was there with his family: Aunt Audrey, thin-lipped and bird-boned and quiet, and their two dirt-smeared sons who ran around the house like crazed pinballs knocking everything over. Uncle Charlie worked construction, a real man's man.

And this was the first holiday Paul had invited his own family to come to the ranch as well. Paul's sister Susan, an interior decorator, had married into money—Don was in the oil business—and they had a son Matthew, who was in high school and who folded his arms across his chest, perpetually annoyed. Justin wasn't used to such din and racket; he was used to having his mother and his grandmother to himself.

At dinner he pretended to be a gentleman, constantly reaching over platters of goose and sweet potatoes and collard greens to refill wine glasses as an excuse to top off his own. His mother talked throughout the meal about everything imaginable, especially about how great it all was, trying in vain to make up for the situation, to lubricate this new family dynamic. Perfect, absolutely perfect, she said of the new Arabian stallion brought from Houston, of the catfish Justin had fried up the night before, of the sky and the weather. Perfect.

"Justin is going underground," his grandmother announced to the table. Her eyebrows rose conspiratorially as she brandished her goblet of apple juice in the air. "He has taken a job with the subway."

"Do him some good," said Uncle Charlie, whose way of dealing with his mother's health was to pretend as if nothing were wrong with her. "Manual labor is better for depression than any drug on the market."

"Justin is not working for the subway. He's still at Harvard," his mother said, always looking for a chance to slip that in, and at that moment Justin realized even though she'd asked him to drop out of graduate school, she knew he wouldn't; she didn't really expect him to. She probably figured it would relieve her from being 'the heavy' if putting his grandmother into a Home was partially his decision too. "And just because someone doesn't have your sensibility, Charlie, doesn't mean they're depressed."

"Don't go taking my words out of context, now. I was just making a general statement about hard work, wasn't I, hon?" he said, turning to his wife, who proceeded to flip his bolo tie over his shoulder to keep it out of the sauce.

His mother mentioned that one of Justin's professors had recently been profiled in the New Yorker, probably hoping this would prod Justin into discussing what he was doing in Studio. But Justin avoided talking about his work, avoided expounding on his newfound conviction that Brutalist architecture—making a virtue of the construction process; leaving the structural and service elements exposed—was not dead. Not everyone called it dead but most did, especially those who did not live within walking distance of the only Le Corbusier building in America, situated on the edge of the campus like a spiraling concrete rabbit hole. Justin's theory was if you gave it time, let the landscape grow lush around such buildings, twisting and unfurling over the steel and concrete, it would work. But he didn't feel like talking about this even though his mother always loved to listen to these theories in part because she didn't understand them or maybe understood they were silly but not to him. He didn't feel like hearing Uncle Charlie call him "art damaged" or an "ineffectual intellectual," which was more or less the opposite of what his uncle meant when he called somebody a "straight shooter."

"And I said to her, I don't like lemons in my beer, in my water, in my goddamn lemonade," his uncle was telling the table, something about an argument with Aunt Audrey, who didn't seem to be listening but rather concentrating on slicing her sons' meat into pieces small enough for a sparrow. Justin's mother smiled at her newly minted husband as if to say, only one more day, endure them for one more day, and we will be alone again with the dogwoods and deer, just the two of us—and a crazy old woman wearing red silk pajamas and a fur coat.

"To the Chinese, the lemon is a symbol of death," Justin told his uncle, ignoring the private look between his mother and Paul, which should have been a look exchanged between his mother and him. It was his ranch, not theirs. His dogwood and his deer and his grandmother and his Hole.

"Key lime pie is not my favorite pie, but it is my favorite name for a pie," his grandmother said. It was the lemon, thought Justin. The lemon made her think of lime.

The more Justin drank, the more contemptuous he became of the family strangers, as he called them, these people who were crowding the dining room and eating with their mouths open. He passed food down the table when asked, his long fingers splayed out beneath platters of green beans with almond slivers, onion casserole, buttermilk biscuits, but the entire meal disgusted him, so much death and gluttony, scraping and masticating.

"This market ain't gonna last forever," Don, Paul's brother, was saying, his napkin tucked into his shirt like a bib. "Especially for big holdings like this. I'm just saying you should consider it."

"Will do. Will do," Paul said. "Although, the decision's not up to me, if you know what I mean." He nodded his head toward Justin's mother. And that's when Justin realized they were discussing the ranch. Paul, who had only been married to his mother for a year, was actually discussing selling the ranch.

Susan was simultaneously yapping his ear off about her son Matthew, about how smart he was, how well he would do in school if only he'd apply himself. "It's all baseball and rock concerts. I really wish I knew what to do with him," she said, fiddling with her gold bangle bracelets. "Maybe you could talk to him. Take him aside and let him know it's possible to be both smart and cool."

Justin got up to leave the table, picking up his china plate stained purple from the cranberry sauce, holding it upright like some kung-fu weapon. "But it isn't possible," he said. "I chose cool."

After washing dishes in the basin sink, scrubbing until his hands were red, Justin walked back to the House of Guns while most of the others ate dessert in the parlor and got drunk. The sky was the still, empty cobalt of winter, almost gray along the horizon, and the rocking chairs on the porch, as if inhabited by ghosts, pitched forward and back with the wind. Paul was out in the pasture walking the Arabian in circles, ankle deep in dead brown grass.

Justin wanted a smoke, but he was out of papers. He found a Gideon Bible in the living room cupboard, God knows where it came from, and ripped out a page from Song of Solomon. He was reminded of a story he'd heard about one of his professors, about how he'd been in a Japanese POW camp with tobacco and nothing to roll it in but a pocket copy of Dante's Inferno, which he smoked page by page, but not before memorizing its every line. Justin supposed it was some sort of sacrilege to smoke the Bible. One of his friends back in Boston called him an aesthetic Catholic, which he considered to be mostly true. He loved the churches, the way they echoed the click clacking of high heels, the way they could be filled with sheaths of velvet and towering gold crosses and endless wooden pews and yet be so empty—all artifice. Like his saint medals, beautiful but helpless hanging against the bones of his chest. Unlike those who lose their faith and secretly pine for it the rest of their lives, Justin did not wish things different. Devotion stole minutes—thoughts and the minutes you used to think them. Thought-minutes he didn't have to spare.

His grandmother came down from the main house to sit with him on the porch as he smoked; she attempted to tuck her legs up under her like a young girl, but her joints would have none of it. The two of them rocked back and forth in unison.

"Who gets the ranch? In your will?" he asked, not turning to look directly at her.

"There is a graveyard, you know, back beyond the grove of Pecans. I don't know who's buried there. Probably just dogs," she said. Justin had scoured every corner of this ranch as a youth and had never noticed a grave marker anywhere near there.

"Do they split it? Mom and Uncle Charlie? Please, try to focus for a minute. They want to sell the ranch. Do you understand what I'm saying?" he asked.

"Talk to Floyd in the morning. Talk to Floyd about it," she said, referring to her dead husband. She told Justin about how the ranch used to be the largest one for miles and how she was so proud to marry Floyd because she liked owning all the land she could possibly see in any direction. She told him how they'd eventually sold off some pieces to pay debts and how she didn't like the family who'd bought the largest share. "They were real Southerners, if you know what I mean. From Alabama. They do things differently there."

Justin dropped the issue of the will. He thought to himself, just let it go, she can't help you anymore. But he laughed at what she said about Alabamians. It was true Texas was not exactly the South, but when you were in New England it became close enough, and so he'd bonded with students from Tennessee and Mississippi as if their hometowns were right next door. Ironically, Justin had never seen wisteria bloom until his first spring in Cambridge, when he thought to himself, so this is what Faulkner was talking about. He believed home was the parts of your past you chose to keep. He wore a straw cowboy hat out to the bar when he was in the mood to get loaded, and people would say to him Texans sure do know how to drink and he would grin and think: just don't ask me how to two-step; I can do it, but like a twelve year-old dancing with his mother.

People in his design program were probably saying he was a drunk, the wild motherfucker in the Western shirt, which wasn't the whole truth although it certainly was some of it; part of him just hoped if he acted crazy, like a loose cannon, when he finally designed something good, they'd say it was brilliant. Maybe that was because, if he was going to fizzle out, and he was, it should be fast like a comet. Maybe he was no different than any other ambitious fuck. Maybe he didn't want to design buildings. Maybe he just wanted to be one. Yes! To be a building! A building that lasts. Except they never really did; they were just the illusion of permanence. But, sometimes, late at night, smoking a cigarette on the porch of the House of Guns, he thought that might be enough.

His grandmother began to doze off in the rocking chair; she looked briefly at him first, before letting her eyes close. This meant he should carry her to bed, which he did, not because he was that strong but because she was that small, eighty-seven pounds. He had no use for people who did not live like this, like he and his grandmother lived, on unspoken understanding. He said loyalty and suspension of judgment were the two qualities he valued most in a friend; what he really meant was he needed someone who could sit beside him on the porch, on the stoop, when the whole craggy world was flooding unbearably in through the Hole in his head, and say nothing.

As he carried his grandmother in his arms—he could feel the

padding of her adult diaper beneath the silk pajamas—through the living room with its exposed brick walls, its shelves lined with dozens of knickknacks and its animal pelt rugs, he thought about his friends in Boston: they would be crowding into David's apartment about then, in their turtleneck ponchos and wool pants, wet boots lined up outside the door covered with the brown slush they'd had to trudge through.

David, who had done his undergrad in anthropology and had an annoying habit of attracting women who were a lot better looking than he was, would be trying to convince everyone to play his old-school Civilizations board game, I'll even let you be the Illyrians. Stella, who was Belgian and in the landscape design program would be taking black and white photographs of everybody with her Yoshica. She liked to capture parts of people, body parts, a calf in stockings, a flexed tricep, a mouth saying "no." And Rachel, the spiky-haired woman whom Justin had been sleeping with on and off, would be watching everything, wondering what she was doing anywhere near a party where so many people were talking about the superstructure and the phantasmagoric and floating signifiers.

Of course, that's not all people talked about, even at Harvard Graduate School of Design parties. They were pretentious, sure, but there was still gossip, talk of the Red Sox and the weather, of being homesick. And then someone would ask, does that mean you'll move back when you're finished? And he would say nonchalantly: no, probably not, nothing to go back to really. Maybe one day I'll buy some land out there. But not now. Definitely not yet. Because the northeast had become something of an addiction; it made him feel as if he needed it, as if it had something he couldn't exactly put his finger on but doubted he could live without. Justin was the ranch—a place where the Hole lurked around every corner—but he was also Harvard; he was also architecture; he also had his own life.

After tucking in his grandmother and hanging her fur coat on a metal hanger in the accordion closet, he didn't go straight to bed but wandered through the house, turning off lights and closing curtains. When he and his mother first moved to the ranch, Justin had insisted on living in the House of Guns. Sometimes, when he was home visiting, he swore he heard tapping on the windows, heard Valerie Valentine tapping to get in, to come inside and make love on the animal pelts like they used to when he was seventeen and felt all grown up. A boy with a man's house. He and Val never had much to say to each other, and Justin thought that was why he'd never entirely forgotten her. Rachel, back in Boston, was capricious and was always trying to tell him how she felt—he was emotionally abusive one day and the love of her life the next—as if she had no filter whatsoever. Valerie never ruined it with words. Valerie understood what he had come to believe: words change nothing. But, then again, Valerie had also left him. Something Rachel never seemed quite able to do. Not that it really mattered one way or the other, he thought, because when he saw his future, he never imagined anyone by his side. Maybe it was melodramatic—so what?— but it was the ranch he imagined as his family when his family was gone.

Justin's grandmother had only moved to the House of Guns within the last few months when Paul decided it was too disturbing to open the bathroom door at night and find an old woman staring at him from an empty claw-foot bathtub. But Justin didn't think she was safe living in the House of Guns by herself, and he imagined this was intentional, another way his mother was pushing him to decide. Or maybe he was overreacting. It was strange how, in some ways, his grandmother was taking Justin's place; and in other ways, he would one day be taking hers.

Barefoot and walking gingerly across the living room floorboards, Justin jerked the lever behind Carlos Fuentes's *The Old Gringo* and pulled the bookcase toward him like a French door. Bordello, dungeon, lair: these were the words that always slipped into his head as splinters of light from the hallway half-heartedly illuminated the ground and rising dust particles of the secret vault, the brooding and threatening shadows. There was the smell of must mixed with metal: the smell of manhood. Every time he opened this door, he felt its power.

As his eyes adjusted to the dark, he reached above his head for the string leading to the light bulb. The room was the size of a large walk-in closet. Cedar walls lined with hunting equipment: camo jackets, orange vests and decoy turkeys. The guns were amazing. His grandfather had made a special freestanding shelf for them in the center of the room, and they were lined up in rows, all pointing 45 degrees upward toward the sky. There was a row of rifles, Remington 700s mostly with a couple of Browning A-bolts, and another row of pistols, all different, antique as well as more modern ones, that his grandfather had acquired at gun shows.

Justin had rarely gone inside this room since his grandfather died, once to show Val, who hated it and had cocked her head as if she were somehow disappointed in him, and once to get a rifle so as to scare away coyotes that had been stalking the cattle at night. And once, earlier that day, to clean the guns. When he'd held one outright, aiming it at the door, his arms and hands shook like a Parkinson's patient, like they had never done before. In the year or so before his grandfather's death, they'd gone hunting every time Justin visited. His mother said his grandfather was using any excuse to get out of the house and away from his ailing wife; the moment she'd stopped making sense was the moment his grandfather stopped listening. But when Justin went out with his grandfather—dove hunting, deer hunting—he had always been a steady shot. His arms definitely never shook like that. Had they?

Justin stood in front of the rack and picked up his favorite—the lightest of the rifles with delicate silver engraving—and remembered one night nine years, just before he'd moved away from the ranch for college. His grandmother had been with him in the House of Guns babbling half-nonsense from the couch, and he went to help her to bed. They padded silently through the living room, Justin's arm circling her waist as she leaned heavily against him, and his grandmother stopped him right there in front of the bookshelf, pointing at it with a persistent finger, pointing, he thought, to the cache of guns behind the bookshelf. They stood there for a while, her body tensed in rebellion against him, until finally he shook his head definitively and she went slack, defeated, let him take her to bed. He'd felt a strange surge of power. And shame at feeling that power. But his grandmother had done something he'd since sworn not to do—waited too long. She had waited to do it until she needed someone else's help.

That night Justin dreamed he was in the Smithsons' famous House of the Future surrounded by its Jetsons-like plastic furniture; he was lying in the middle of the floor, which was actually the ground since the house was built around a garden, looking up at the ceiling as it curved away from him. Like footage from a time-lapse camera, tree branches steadily grew until they were stymied by the walls and the ceiling, forced to bend their way back downward, brushing up against him, wrapping and suffocating him. He was being freed from the need to breathe.

In the morning, after polishing his boots in the bathroom, Justin knocked on the door to his grandmother's bedroom. Again and again, until finally he said, "Okay, I'm coming in." She wasn't there. Her red silk pajamas were folded neatly at the end of the bed. He yelled for her, walking toward the closed bathroom door, but nothing. He stood for a moment before opening it, images lit up behind his eyes: her slight, wrinkled body collapsed in the tub, on the floor, the Hole having swallowed her whole. But when he finally pushed open the door, there was nobody in the tub or on the floor. She had simply disappeared.

As Justin walked out onto the porch of the House of Guns, he could see his mother standing at the screen door of the main house, drying her palms along her faded Levis. The wrinkles on her cheeks ran vertically giving her face a thinner appearance, and she frowned at him as he walked down the path toward her. "Got yourself an escapee?" she asked.

"You act as if this isn't unusual," he replied.

"It isn't," she said. "She needs to be in a Home where someone can watch her all the time, Justin. I just can't do it."

"Are you selling the ranch?"

"What?" she asked, looking down at him from the edge of the porch.

"I heard Paul last night at dinner," he said. "So just tell me. When she dies, are you selling it?"

"Justin, don't be ridiculous," she said, matter-of-factly. "Even if we wanted to, we can't. They left you fifty-one percent."

"Of the main house and the House of Guns?"

"I hate it when you call it that."

"How was she even capable of...?"

"It was your grandfather, actually, before he died. He said a boy without a father ought to have something. If it's ever sold, you'll be the one who does it," she said, her face suddenly emptied of expression. The look, he thought, that she got when her mind had already moved beyond the present moment and had no more use for it. "I'd suggest heading toward the hay field."

He started jogging down the dirt road covered with a cinnamon-brown silt, not exactly worrying about his grandmother so much as thinking about her, knowing she'd be all right. Even if she wasn't.

As he ran, he imagined the Hole as the inverse of what it really was, imagined his grandmother had become too full of wisdom to communicate with mere mortals, the bursting flesh of a plum from skin too tight to keep it. And somehow this made him think again of Valerie Valentine and how she would sit in his kitchen and scrape the rind of her melon clean with a spoon, how sensuous he thought that was and how innocent he'd been to think it was enough. Justin liked to say he didn't believe in the pornography of detail, but that wasn't really true. All architects knew details were everything.

He rounded the bend of the dirt road and spotted his grandmother teetering along. She was dressed to the nines in pumps, a pillbox hat, a leather valise gripped firmly in her blue-veined hand as she made her way to freedom.

"Where are you going?" he asked. He had caught up with her. He knew exactly where she was going yet, breaking their rule to understand in silence, he had asked anyway.

"I left a note," she said. "Didn't you get my note?"

"No note."

"I wrote it in my head," she said. She stopped to look around, surprised, then sat on a flat rock by the side of the road and placed the valise on her lap. She crossed her legs as if she were a young woman in a train station somewhere. She motioned for him to sit beside her and he did. "It said: It's important to leave while you can," she told him. "That's what the note said, I think. Something like that."

As she leaned toward him, her valise slid off her lap and the latch popped open. Justin flinched as a flash of metal appeared. But it was only a picture frame with an autographed photo of Gene Kelly. A dozen or so other items tumbled out and onto the ground, and Justin helped her to gather them back up. Plastic baggies stuffed with figs and pretzels. A wooden set of rosary beads. She picked up a stack of papers, scrambling for them with trembling hands. They were letters. He looked closer and realized they were his letters to her. He loved her for that.

"Here," she said. "I have these legal documents for the lawyer. But we must hurry. Mr. Taylor closes at four."

Neither of them moved. They both stared straight ahead for a long time, looking out at the brush and the barbed wire. A couple of crows flew overhead. He felt both exalted and wretched. At some point, Justin thought he would ask her if she'd like some migas for breakfast, and he would tell her, like any good friend, that she should eat something to give her strength before starting out again. But first he just sat there beside her as silent and still and expressionless as the buildings he loved so much: Trellick Tower, Robin Hood Gardens, La Tourette. He was blank. He was a found object. He was glass and steel. He was concrete. He was the poetry of the every day. And he would be beautiful in time when the vines and climbers twisted and unfurled and grew up lush around him.

for joshua

~The Renaissance Man~

Betty Jean Tucker

What Screamersville needed to get through the Depression, Judge Scoggins decided, was a Renaissance man. It was expressed as a joke, but his son, called Junior by everyone who knew him, took it seriously and declared that he would be that Renaissance man.

First, he prowled through some relevant books in his father's law library and came away from his research with a vague idea of great multi-talented iconic figures who wowed the rich Medici in sixteenth-century Italy. He could be Michelangelo and Shakespeare and a doctor and a preacher if that's what the hard times required.

Now in his late twenties, he was generally considered to be a rustic dilettante. His father thought him brilliant but would admit to his being "different." Once, in a truth-serum mood, he had speculated that Dr. Morgan had circumcised the wrong part of his son's anatomy.

The first person with whom Junior shared his vision of himself in a new role was Miss Rosa Appleby, the retired schoolteacher spinster, who listened to him in amusement and pointed out that he had no credentials for such a lofty aspiration and that the Sistine Chapel was awesome but could not put food on the table.

He was not one whit discouraged, remembering his childhood as an artist and businessman. He recalled his habit of doodling on everything, a practice which his mother praised. It led him to raid the attic to rescue some of the old drawings. One of them, a sketch of the old courthouse with its two massive Corinthian columns, was, he decided, a bit amateurish but showed promise. He remembered then that his childhood ambition to be an artist had resulted in his and Craig Smith's operating a vending stand to sell his art. The venture had been short-lived because he had served his customers drinks from his father's liquor cabinet. He knew that the liquor had been made at Runt

Wilson's still in the woods behind Pete's Pond out in the country, but the brew was tempting as it lay like liquid diamonds in his mother's heavy crystal decanter. He and his customers had become tipsy and wallowed in a pleasant glow until somebody told the judge and ruined the enterprise.

Now here he was, caught in the deprivations of a national depression, with a lingering regret over the loss of artistic talent that might have elevated him to the status of a savior figure in Screamersville. A struggling little town in the Alabama Black Belt, it had kept its pioneer name that reflected the wildness of its early history. The town was tame now. Gone were the gun battles, saloon stabbings, and the wails of women in the night. But as the Depression relentlessly pushed the people into poverty, there was a sense of screaming, silent but boiling, just under the surface of everyday life. Although Junior's own personal life as the son of the town's most powerful and respected family was less threatened than others, he felt the pain and desperation of their lives.

His thoughts turned to writing. He knew that he could not be Shakespeare. But he liked to write and savored the saying that the pen is mightier than the sword. He knew that he could write because he had a publication to his credit. He had entered an essay contest in *Grit Magazine* and won second place with his portrayal of his life as the son of a distinguished judge. His father tried to be proud but was embarrassed at the self-conscious erudition, the piling on of polysyllabic words like "magnanimous behavior," "mellifluous voice," and "prognosticative skills." Back he went to recover the old yellowed magazine from the attic. Reading it again after all those years, he winced at the hey-look-at-me diction and wondered why he had ever thought he could write.

So he took his plan for being a Renaissance man back to the drawing board, determined to use his artistic instincts as a broad humanities base on which to build a career as a doctor. Surely that profession would allow him the opportunity to do enormous good in a chaotic time of great need.

The next semester at the University of Alabama found him in chemistry and physics classes, which he hated, and in an anatomy class, which intrigued him and led him to apprentice himself to a friend of the Judge, a Tuscaloosa doctor with a practice in gynecology. A sense of euphoria settled over him as he trailed his doctor mentor through office visits, examinations, diagnoses, surgeries, and home visits. And he developed a special relationship with Matilda, Dr. Strait's wooden mannequin, a shapely full-figured form with intricate anatomically correct insides.

With a keen scientific interest, he studied the coiled intestines, the stomach, the colon, kidneys, liver, appendix — all painted a ghastly pink, which he admired in the belief that the color fairly represented the look of real organs. He was excited to learn about female genitalia, which had been a fascinating mystery to him. The positioning of the womb, the fallopian tubes, the ovaries, the vagina and the clitoris became emblazoned on his mind like a map.

The magic of reproduction stirred in him a purely medical interest, but there was nothing scientific about his feeling when Matilda was all closed up, and the seductively curved hips and the rounded breasts reminded him of Melly Landers. The memory of Melly fired his imagination with a lust which burned even brighter as he watched Dr. Strait examine his patients' breasts.

The elderly doctor, encouraged by Junior's eager interest, seized the opportunity to teach and demonstrated the procedure for feeling a woman's breasts to detect lumps that might be cancerous. It was the first time Junior had heard the word "cancer," and he listened intently to the doctor's explanation that women were vulnerable to breast cancer, which was most often fatal. He impressed upon his young assistant how important it was to detect the disease in its early stages in order to save lives.

The phrase "save lives" suggested a role for the Renaissance man as a savior figure. He could not have been more inspired if a heavenly chorus had called to him with the summons to "Go forth." Under Dr. Strait's watchful eye, Junior performed several breast exams and felt buoyed by the veteran doctor's praise. The light bulb in his brain blazed with a sudden conviction. He would be a breast examiner specialist. To that end, he purchased a black bag, a stethoscope, needles and syringes, tongue depressors, a blood pressure apparatus, cotton balls, bandaging gauze, rubbing alcohol, and a watch with a second hand. To make himself look slightly older, like a reputable physician, he bought a pair of thick lens glasses and applied white shoe polish to the edges of his hair. When his image in the mirror assured him that he looked trustworthy, he set off for Fifteenth Street.

He chose his first house carefully, stopping in front of a modest little white wooden house with neat green shutters, a brick walk, and blooming camellias splaying a pink glow everywhere. He almost lost his nerve when no one answered his knock immediately and was about to turn away when a thin young woman wearing a becoming blue gingham dress opened the door.

"Good morning," he said, with what he hoped was his most engaging smile. "I'm Leonard Armstrong, one of Dr. Martin Cox's medical students at the University. I'm working on a project which I would like to talk with you about. May I come in?"

She was puzzled and a little reluctant, but she did let him in and listened to his carefully prepared speech.

"I know it must seem strange," he said, "to have a doctor make a house call without being summoned. But I assure you this is a perfectly legitimate clinical research project conducted by interns under the supervision of the medical college. The study has been commissioned by the state health department in the interest of locating and identifying women with breast cancer in order to treat it early on and save lives."

He could tell she was uncomfortable. "I don't know what cancer is," she said, her cheeks going slightly pink.

"That's understandable. Women have been dying for years with this disease without knowing what was wrong with them." He did the best he could with describing symptoms and treatment, emphasizing the importance of being examined and evaluated early.

"What do I have to do?" she asked.

"Three things. I'll take your vital signs, help you fill out a medical history form, and then examine your breasts — the same as in a doctor's office."

"I don't have money to pay you." She seemed ashamed.

"The service is absolutely free. We know that the Depression is keeping people from needed medical care."

With his little black bag, the professional demeanor of a real doctor, and the quiet cooperation of his patient, he undertook the examination.

He pulled an unsteady chair beside the bed where she lay with her dress open and was caught in the snares of his dueling impulses: The perfection of the breasts registered in his mind as seductive beauty, but any arousal was kept at bay by his unexpected empathy for the patient, who was even younger than he. Her body language —the rigid stillness of her body, the turning away of her face, and the refusal to look at him — made him keenly aware of her painful embarrassment, her struggle to endure the violation of her privacy to get peace of mind about her health. When his hands began their exploratory movements, she closed her eyes, and a little frown creased her brow. His fingers were immune to lust as he silently commanded himself not to find any lumps. When he was finished, she sat up, buttoning her dress, and asked, "Am I all right, Doctor?"

"You're just perfect. No suspicious knots or lumps."

She smiled then, her lips trembling ever so slightly and her green eyes dancing in the happy color of spring. "I'm so relieved," she admitted. "I was worried about the baby."

In amazement, he watched her pat her absolutely flat stomach. "You're going to have a baby?" he asked.

"Yes," she said happily. "When you told me about cancer, I was so afraid that I might not be able to nurse the baby."

"How far along are you?"

When she told him six months, he expressed concern over her lack of weight gain and urged her to eat more.

"Oh, I have always been skinny," she told him brightly. "I get enough to eat. We have a good little garden in the back yard."

He was skeptical, but the irrepressible joy she felt over her maternal expectations gave his own spirits a lift. He philosophized that the little china doll of a woman, so fragile and pretty, would defy the Depression, meet hardship with tough love, and glory in her woman's role of reproduction. He thought her to be beautiful — truly innocent and brave. Reluctantly he left her, but he had the names of several women in the neighborhood who might be interested in participating in the study.

At the end of the extraordinary day, he felt fulfilled. On one level, he knew very well that he was a con man who would be exposed and punished eventually. But on another level, he knew that his behavior, though originally deriving from impure motives, was a sincerely noble attempt to save lives. Not once had he thought of the voluptuous Melly.

But she forced her way into his dreams that night, clawing viciously like a yowling cat at his face while he tore at her clothes to get at the wicked breasts whose image had tormented his libido for months. Walking her home after prayer meeting, he had caved in to potent sixteen-year-old urges, and in the shadow of the church he tried some ill-advised moves which sent her into near hysteria. He awoke in a sweat and did not understand why the image that remained in his mind was the church steeple.

For the next month he accumulated a lifetime's worth of images that bedeviled his mind sleeping and waking. While he honed his skills as pseudo-physician, his memory bank bulged with experiences that brought the Depression up close and personal. More bitter than quinine was the plight of Mildred LeGrande, who opened the door to his knock, grabbed his hands and pulled him in eagerly.

Mistaking him for an undertaker, she led him directly to a bedroom, where the only piece of furniture was a handsome four-poster bed burdened with the lifeless body of her husband. A petite woman with black hair pulled severely back into a bun, she had the flawless delicate look of a porcelain doll and moved with practiced grace. She called him monsieur and spoke with an accent, asking him what information he required. When they both realized that theirs was a case of mistaken identity, he explained that he had been called to a different patient in the neighborhood and got the wrong address. The mistake made him uneasy, and he wanted to leave, but she begged him to stay. "Just until the funeral people come, *Monsieur*. It is just that I am afraid to be alone with the dead."

He reassured her. "I think you are a brave person. You have bathed and dressed him, and look at the careful way you have brushed his hair." And they stood and stared down at the corpse, a handsome man with black hair tinged with grey and an elaborately curved handlebar mustache.

"You think I did good, *Monsieur?*"

"Yes, indeed."

With the intimacy that could only be understood by lovers, she leaned down and stroked the cold cheek of her dead love and murmured in a silken whisper. "Now I dance for you, *mon chéri*, the last time."

With that, the black-clad figure rose on tiptoes in her steel-toed ballet shoes and raised her arms above her head in an arc. With no music but the memories in her head, she danced in celebration of the joy and sorrow of her life. Her audience had no trouble imagining that the beginning of the dance, with its quick, fluid movements and the happy expression on the dancer's face, represented the meeting of the lovers in the shadow of the Eiffel Tower during the Great War. Then the movements suggested the "Wedding March," with the tiny hands pulling love out of the air and holding it over her heart. He lost the thread of her story then and gave himself over to the beauty of the dance with its magic. He did not want it to end, but the dance slowed into the sense of funereal march as the expressive hands and arms reached upward as if giving up the loved one to eternity.

Spent, she stood at the foot of the bed and spoke: "*Au revoir, mon chéri.*" The ruffled sheer fabric at her neck rose and fell. Her eulogy had not been macabre; it had produced an emotional power that moved both of them.

"Please to come with me now, *Monsieur* Doctor," she urged, taking his hand and leading him through the door, which she closed with a click of finality.

In the living room, standing in a pool of October sunlight, she looked older, he thought, noting the fine web of lines around her mouth and eyes. He watched her walk to a scarred brown suitcase sitting beside the front door and change to a pair of sensible black walking shoes. A strong sense of emptiness emanated from the oppressive space around him, unoccupied except for a massive breakfront at one end of the room. It was much more elegant than the one in his own home. Seeing him studying the piece of furniture, she took from it the only thing there — a sterling silver statuette of a young ballerina.

"For my role in the national ballet's performance of *The Nutcracker*, she explained, holding it to her chest like a baby. "The ballet was the heart of my life until a handsome young American soldier showed me what real happiness is," she confided. "We were happy, even though his life took him into the mines to earn a living." Then bitterness claimed her voice. "The mine controlled our lives until it closed, and then the Depression came and it was the beginning of the end. *C'est la vie.*"

He was too awkward with words to know how to comfort her. "What will you do now?"

The question stirred within her the hatred of implacable foes that could not be grappled with in fair fight. Her voice was a vicious claw: "America is a lie. It promises the dream, then kills it. I think God does not love America, or else why would he send this cruel Depression. I say the Lord's Prayer and choke on my anger."

Suddenly, she was reciting the first phrases of the prayer in French. She spat out the words in contempt, her face contorted and her grey eyes enormous: "*Notre Pere qui es aux cieux / Que ton nom soit sanctifite/ Que ton regne vienne.*" His ego swelled at her assumption that he would understand French.

She shifted into English for the words "Thy will be done," words that she now clearly despised. She flung her fury into the empty room, crying, "*Mon Dieu, Mon Dieu*, why was it your will? Why? He was my world." Her passionate orgy of grief reverberated in the mausoleum of a room.

He was relieved when the undertaker knocked and brought back into focus the mundane world with its insistence on getting the dead satisfactorily buried. "I'm Walter Boswell, with Fleet's Mortuary, Mrs. LeGrande. If you will just show us the deceased."

Made calm by their appearance, she busied herself with assisting them, and when the stretcher with its burden left the house, she picked up the suitcase and they followed the corpse to the waiting hearse. As the door closed, she called, "*Dieu vous garde, mon chéri.*"

"Where are you going?" he asked as the hearse moved away from the curb.

"I go home to France, *Monsieur* Doctor. *Au revoir.*"

He watched her stride purposefully down the street. He would see her in his dreams, striding away down the street or performing her dance of death with consummate grace.

Many disturbing scenes intruded into his sleeping and waking hours. He might be in the process of examining a breast and find himself thinking of the woman with the goat. He had walked into her house with his black bag and found himself confronting the Depression face to face in the form of four barefooted, ragged big-eyed children so malnourished they moved in a cloud of lethargy. The woman herself was a ghost of a human, clutching a newborn baby, which cried weakly and gnawed its fist.

He forgot his purpose in response to her overwhelming need. "Is there anything I can do for you?" he had asked.

A faint tic worried the corner of her flat lips. "Do you know how to milk a goat?" she asked, clearly expecting nothing. "I can't nurse the baby, and somebody gave me a nanny goat."

He would have tried anything. "Well, I have milked a cow, so I'd be glad to try. Where is the goat?"

The tallest child, a ten-year-old with a grotesque harelip, left the room and was back immediately, leading an uncooperative animal with a full udder in desperate need of milking. It eyed the doctor with a malevolent yellow glare and chewed mightily on a piece of brown paper bag.

"Get me a pan with some water and a pail for the milk," he directed the boy. The child moved quickly to the kitchen and returned with the water and pail. The children eased forward to watch the drama. "Put the halter around her neck, stand in front of her, and try to make her stand still," he told the boy.

"She'll butt me," the reluctant child said.

"Maybe. But the baby needs milk." And with that, he went to his knees, held the pan of water under the goat and washed each teat carefully.

"Aah," the boy said, finally understanding and relishing his role at center stage.

With the mother hovering behind him to watch, he showed them how to pull on the teat, occasionally pushing a teat upward into the under for a better flow of milk. When he got the milk squirting into the pail with a regular rhythm, the children were amazed, and the mother urged him to let her try.

The goat, no doubt relieved to be rid of her overload of milk, behaved well, and the mother was just as relieved that she had learned how to get the precious milk.

Junior prepared to leave, thinking wryly that he would be forever cured of his fascination for breasts, having found no sexual excitement whatsoever in a goat's teats.

The pathetic little group followed him to the door with gratitude for the miracle of milk. But they scattered frantically with the shriek of "Nanny goat is eating the Bible!"

He could find no humor or hope in another instance when he had to attend to an immediate need. Someone had given him the name of Gloria Pettway, who lived in the Forest Hill subdivision on the west side of town. When he explained his mission, she agreed readily, but she made it clear that she expected a quid pro quo. A dumpy little woman in her sixties, she had a round face and a sweet smile which was affixed to her face like a beatific signature. She smiled through the medical history forms, through vital signs (even when told that her blood pressure was 185 over 95) and through the examination. She was indifferent when he found no signs of cancer. Her purpose clearly was the fulfillment of the promise of a favor he had agreed to.

Buttoning her housecoat, she led him to a bedroom. It was dominated by a hospital bed in which resided a huge grown man, perhaps forty years old. Nothing moved except his eyes. Her smile broadened as she kept up a croon: "Here we are, precious. Everything will be all right now. Mama's here. The doctor is here and the world is good. Are you hungry, little one? Soon Mama will feed you strawberries and cream if you are good for the doctor. And you will be good, won't you? You are your mama's precious one, the apple of her eye." All the while she chattered she was stroking his cheek, brushing his hair back from his forehead, wiping the saliva from a corner of his mouth, smoothing the sheet over his mound of stomach and immobile legs.

Junior was troubled at the thought that she would expect him to do something medical for the man. But such was not the case. She motioned for him to join her at the bedside. "This is Doctor Leonard, Luv," she said to her son. "He's going to shave you today, pet. Isn't that wonderful? You know, Mama has always said the Lord giveth and the Lord taketh away. Well, the Lord took our dear Mr. Chambers, but see, He has given us Doctor Leonard." She turned to Junior, and the baby talk gave way to her adult voice as she showed him the table containing the items for shaving. There were an antique Wedgewood bowl and pitcher, a shaving mug containing soap and a well-worn brush, a bath cloth and towel, a bib, a straight razor and the leather strop for sharpening the razor. While she put the bib on the patient, Junior checked the long dull blade of the razor and began slapping it against the leather strop. Almost immediately, the patient reacted to the slapping sound. It began as a low guttural moan and grew into the primitive sound of a wounded animal. The flesh of his face had the bloated look of a balloon.

When Junior looked at the woman for some explanation, she smiled her answer across the room. "Don't be alarmed. He always does that."

"What is wrong with him?"

"He was born an idiot."

"How long has he been an invalid?"

"All of his life. I have been blessed." And the smile did not waver.

When the slapping noise stopped, the man's sounds subsided. After Junior had wet and lathered the face, he reached for the razor and held it up to the light to check on the sharpness.

"Don't," she said.

"What?" he asked, but then he saw the man's eyes. Enormous and protuberant, the grey eyes glistened and flamed out in terror, bespeaking a primal fear, desperate and wild.

"Why is he so afraid?"

"He associates the razor with pain. Mr. Chambers was so good to us, but his hands trembled and sometimes he cut Lane."

With that information, his own hands were none too steady. He tried not to look at the terrified eyes, but the fear was so palpable he was drawn into the terror. He felt the pain as though it were his own when the distraction of the eyes caused him to nick the jawline under the thick, stiff stubble. Then he was dealing with blood and lather, as well as the turbulent agitation of the bulging eyes following him.

The mother ministered to the stormy-eyed creature. She picked up his hand and kissed it, saying "Sh, sh, sh" in a low, quieting tone. "It'll be all right. The doctor made a mistake. He's sorry, Luv. He's almost finished, and you're looking so handsome."

Finally it was over and he escaped. But he couldn't keep the image of those feverish wild eyes out of his mind. He never wanted to go through that again. In fact, he had begun to question his mission to save lives through cancer detection. And then something happened to make him rethink his effort to be a Renaissance man.

One day he stopped his car in front of the shabbiest house in a shabby neighborhood, mentally weighing the yard's oppressive mass of overgrown vegetation smelling of dank heat and pelting rain. Azaleas intruded on hollies, Lady Banks roses ran rampant, clogging a rotting flowerbed, and a camellia bush struggled to birth a delicate pink bloom. It was as if the Depression had turned the landscape into a wasteland. Debris and fallen oak leaves littered the ground. The scene mirrored his own psychic twilight. "Drive on, fool," he told himself, but he trudged on toward the door as if challenged, one more time, to test his fate.

With foreboding, he knocked loudly on the paint-peeling derelict of a door. When a woman opened it, he thought of her as a human derelict. Tall, at almost six feet, she had the skin tone of a consumptive, iron-gray hair, and yellow green eyes that looked as if they had seen hell fire. She was emaciated, but her gauntness could not hide the swollen, bloated look of her body. Even her face looked puffy. When she let him in, he was struck by an ominous silence, but he plunged ahead with the sudden conviction that it might be his last chance to save a life.

She listened to him mutely, fidgeting with a torn ruffle on her stained apron. When he had finished, she ventured a timid, "Does it hurt?"

"Do you mean the examination or the cancer?"

"Both," she replied.

"Well, the exam won't hurt. In fact, if you pay attention to the way I examine you, you can do it yourself in the future."

"But the cancer?"

"You may not feel pain initially, but pain will come and worsen as the disease advances."

Her eyes clouded as though she didn't know how to proceed. "Do you want me to lay down, or…"

And then, to his consternation, that still silence that he had mistrusted migrained into an explosion as a huge lumberjack of a man leaped from a high wingback chair that had concealed him from view, positioned as it was with the back toward the living room. He had evidently listened to the conversation with his blood boiling. In two strides, he was confronting them, his shaggy rust-red hair falling over one bloodshot eye and his soiled khaki pants unzipped over a ballooning belly.

He tore into his wife first, jerking her to face him and slapping her with a force that reddened her pale face. "Can't wait to jump in bed, can you? I have to beat hell out of you to get you in bed and here you are, ready to spread your legs for any peckerwood that comes along."

She mustered courage enough to defend herself. "He's a doctor," she exclaimed. "I'm sick and you won't take me to a doctor."

He raised his hand again. But he ridiculed her instead. "You got to be the dumbest woman ever lived. A guy shows up in a white coat carrying a black bag and you believe he's a doctor. Before you know it, he'll be selling you the Brooklyn Bridge."

When he turned to Junior, he was a fireball of redneck fury. "You ain't a bit more a doctor than I am a angel. Why ain't nobody heard of this so-called program from the health department?"

Junior was not macho in the best of times, and he was shamefully intimidated, but he stood tall and thrust out his chest, hoping that it would not cave in from the big man's fist. "We're in a Depression. There was just not enough money for the health department to mail out notices. This is a legitimate program, and if you touch me I'll have the police on you so fast it'll make your head spin."

The man balled his fist, and Junior braced himself for a blow. But it didn't come. The woman placed her hand on the fist and said calmly, "No, Jason. You'll go to prison if you're arrested again."

The fist remained clinched, but the man did not swing. Instead, he hit Junior with a barrage of cursing and invective so vicious it would have stopped an eighteen-wheeler in overdrive. He ended his diatribe with a triumphant slur: "Now get yore sorry ass out of my house, coming in here like God's gift to women with the gall to mess with a man's wife's titties. You a pore excuse for a man."

And Junior was about ready to agree with him. Any momentary Alamo kind of bravado had turned into sincere regret that he had ever donned a white coat and tried to save a life. Right then, all he wanted was to save his own skin from a shellacking. To that end, he accepted the man's invitation to leave, and he did so without qualms about valor and honor. The man slammed the door after him with a jar that rattled the hinges.

Junior was halfway to his car when the woman called to him. She rushed down the path to him, saying breathlessly, "Please come back tomorrow. He won't be here. Please, please."

He could not resist her pleading and obvious terror and reluctantly agreed to return.

That night, nightmares torpedoed his sleep as he struggled to free himself from a vast spider web coated with a dark syrup as sticky as glue. Awake in the bright glare of a sun trying to warm a cold November day, he pretended sleep until his roommate left for classes. Sitting on the side of his bed, shivering in the unheated room, he reviewed his situation and ultimately reached the conclusion that he had to go to the woman. He refused to think of the possibility that his nemesis might be there.

She let him in with the quick reassurance that Jason would not be at home until night. He had mercifully found a small job.

With both feeling uncomfortable in the clandestine nature of their meeting, they quickly filled out the form with her supplying the information and him writing it down. Her name was Amanda King and he was jolted to learn that she could not write her name. The "X" on the line for her signature was like a mute sigh of grief. He ached for her in her naked embarrassment.

Her vital signs were all over the place, danger signals in every negative reading. How could he possibly help her? How to rescue her from a pending stroke or heart attack or the TB he suspected or the ritual abuse by a madman husband? Her needs were so great and pervasive that he approached the breast examination with dread. He had examined the breasts of thirty-two women, and with each one he shared their elation at the absence of cancer. But this time he knew in his heart that the odds were against a successful outcome. She lay on the bed, and there was in her posture and in her eyes a childlike innocence, a rare kind of trust. Never did a lover fondle a breast with such devotion as he lavished on his clinical analysis. The flesh yielded to his touch as the fingers tested every inch of tissue without encountering any alien matter. He relaxed, straightened his back, and smiled. She could not read a word, but she could read the message in his smile, and he could read the hope in her eyes.

He moved to the other breast, and almost immediately his finger recoiled from a lump the size of a big plum. With his fingers resting on the spot, he looked at her and realized that she had heard the sound of the death knell. A tear slid gently down her cheek and she turned her face to the wall.

He tried to comfort her, but he was seized with a sense of urgency that propelled him into persuading her to go to a doctor. He had made an accurate diagnosis, but he had no power to save her. So he did the best he could. He took her to Dr. Strait. And there in the little office where he had flirted with Matilda, he confessed in private to his mentor what he had been doing and why.

A man of science with little patience for the vagaries of the psyche, the doctor did not know if this son of his old classmate was a lunatic or a well-meaning eccentric. He didn't waste his time analyzing Junior. Together they did a meticulous examination, which the patient endured with emotionless calm. Dr. Strait gave her a three-month supply of medicine for her high blood pressure and made arrangements to perform a lumpectomy to remove the growth.

Junior paid for the doctor's visit and the pending surgery, then carried her home. She assured him that her grown daughter, who lived nearby, would take care of her during and after the surgery. He gave her a wrinkled twenty-dollar bill and felt guilty that in the end all he could do was to give money. Dr. Strait had been mortified by Junior's perversion of the medical profession, but he had amended his sharp criticism with the declaration that his young apprentice had almost certainly saved a life.

But Junior took little joy in the compliment, knowing that his role as a Renaissance man was over. It seemed to him that the manifold hardships wrought by the implacable Depression were overwhelming. And so he went home to Screamersville, where his parents pretended to believe an invented story that was not nearly so strange as the truth.

Daily, for a week, he communed with nature from the bank of Coon's Creek, feeding fat worms on his fishing pole to indifferent catfish. Then the letter came. It contained a hundred dollar bill and a page of explanation. Dr. Strait was returning the money Junior had paid for Amanda's surgery. Jason King had beaten his wife to death when she told him that she was going to have an operation. The man of medicine did not conceal his bitterness. "Where is God," he wrote, "when such heinous things happen? This damn Depression is going to destroy us all."

The guilt Junior grappled with then sent him to the Bible. He left off fishing and devoured the book, searching for the answer to the question the doctor had flung at him about the existence and compassion of God. His total immersion in the orgy of reading troubled his father, and his mother made him hot tea with chamomile and repeatedly checked his brow. His reading was a poultice for his painful disquiet, and he gradually reclaimed his faith, which had been anemic at the time of his baptism at age twelve.

He took a break and went back to the creek bank with his fishing pole. He was there primarily to reflect and did not expect to catch anything. But almost immediately his worm-baited line jerked as if a fish had accepted an invitation to dinner. Junior responded with a true fisherman's excitement and hauled up a hefty catfish with its tail flapping desperately. Once he had his hands on the fish, he felt a white calm settle over him. "Hey, fish," he said. "Long time no see." To his amazement, the fish abruptly stopped struggling, and Junior could swear the fish's eye blinked at him.

In a flash, his mind conjured up a scene at the Sea of Galilee where Christ's first disciples, Andrew and Peter, left their trade as fishermen to follow Jesus as fishers of men. Junior recognized his call. "I hear you, God," he assured his creator, thrilling at a surge of power in his voice. He thought of the old prophet Isaiah bowing to his God and saying, "Here I am. Send me." Tenderly, he freed the fish from the hook and eased it back into the water.

Then the ex-Renaissance man got the second chance he was praying for when the Baptist minister succumbed to tuberculosis and had to be quarantined. The way was clear for Junior to make his debut on the spiritual stage. His road-to-Damascus moment welled into a rhapsodic messianic conviction that demanded expression. At the Wednesday night prayer meeting, he spoke and prayed with such pious passion that the deacons hired him on the spot to be their interim pastor. His heart was afire with the desire to save souls, an even loftier aspiration than healing the body.

For his first Sunday behind the pulpit, he dressed in his black winter suit with its faint odor of mothballs and slicked down his usually unruly brown hair with hair tonic. He had lost weight, but he felt that his slim frame was totally apropos for the lean times and did not worry about his drooping trousers. He hoped that he looked like a man of God as he sat stiffly on the little pine bench behind the pulpit.

It seemed an interminable time for the prayers to be prayed, for the collection plates to be passed for the meager offerings, and for the ten-member choir to sing praises to the Lord. To his surprise, he discovered that he had a pleasant enough baritone voice and joined in the singing, keeping time with his foot. He came out strong on the "wonder working power" of the "blood of the lamb" and felt invigorated by the old familiar hymns, whose lyrics now seemed to him to be poetry of the highest order. Finally, Mr. Otis and Miss Carolyn ended the musical part of the service, and the pulpit was his.

Deliberately, as if on stage, he placed on the stand the Judge's silver pocket watch, assuring the congregation that his sermon would end precisely at twelve o'clock, even if he were in mid-sentence.

To satisfy their curiosity, he assured them immediately that they were looking at a new Junior Scoggins, now a man of God transformed by his call from on high. He judiciously referred only vaguely to the role of the winking catfish as the instrument of divine will. Swiftly, he moved into the darkness of the Depression blighting their lives. "Look," he instructed, dramatically thrusting his hand toward the bare windows. "That's a bleak gray winter landscape outside, isn't it? It kind of matches the misery of our lives and makes us wonder if things will ever be better. Now, you know me. I'm not a wise man, but I have read the Bible, and I know that God lets bad things happen to good people sometimes. Great thinkers and theologians have written eloquently, trying to explain why this is so. But today I am not going to try to explain why God has allowed us to be subject to such hardship and deprivation. I don't know why Eilean and Raymond's little twin boys were born dead; I don't know why money is so scarce that Mr. Jemmerson had to close the hardware store, or why some of our ladies have had to take in washing.

"I don't know the why of these things. But I don't have to. What we all need to know is what to do about it. Since we are all believers here, we can pray for God to change things. And we know that He will heed our prayers eventually." He leaned toward the podium, gripping it until his knuckles whitened. "But the key to our dilemma right now is to get our mindset right. And the way to do that is first to get rid of the frustration and desperation sent by the devil to snare us into the blazing fires of hell. We've got to be like Christ and say, 'Get thee behind me, Satan!'

"We may be tempted to despair like David crying out that he has eaten ashes like bread and mingled his drink with weeping. And we may have an answering cry of the blood when we remember that poem of the old blind poet where he expresses his anguish that God has taken his sight just when he is on fire to write in service to his God." He changed his lofty, emotional tone for a casual aside. "Now you're probably wondering what Junior Scoggins knows about that great writer John Milton. Well, I don't mean to try to sound learned, but I remembered that poem from my sophomore literature class at the University of Alabama several years ago. Even as an indifferent underclassman, I was struck by Milton's conclusion in the poem that God doesn't need Milton, that 'they also serve who only stand and wait.' So the great poetic genius learned to wait, and before Milton died he had written those monumental works, *Paradise Lost* and *Paradise Regained*.

"So what we have to do is resist the desperation. We may feel like we have lost our little paradise here in Screamersville, but we can regain it if we keep the faith and wait for God's delivery." Gratified that no one was nodding off, he launched off in the heart of his message, the haunting story of Job, driven wretched by the contest between Satan and God. He discovered, happily, that he could not only sing, but he could act too.

Seized by an impulsive desire to reenact the book of Job, he abandoned his written notes on the pulpit and strode before the congregation. He gave a decent impersonation of the majestic God and a convincing portrayal of a strutting Satan proclaiming that he had come "from going to and fro in the earth and from walking up and down it," He managed some rustic drama in the initial conflict in which God accepted Satan's challenge to test Job. Then he was first one and then the other of the messengers who reported the calamities that befell Job. He gave short shrift to the dialog of the three false friends, having found that part of the book tedious and boring.

Mindful of his theme, he depicted Job's joyous reconciliation with God and the restoration of his prosperity. He relished the happy-ever-after ending, emphasizing that Job had kept the faith, had waited and endured unspeakable suffering and was rewarded with a hundred and forty more years of life.

He flipped his Bible open and told them, "We are not as perfect as Job. We are God's children, though, and he will take care of us." Again he consulted his Bible, turning the tissue thin paper to read from Isaiah: "and therefore will the Lord wait, that he may be gracious unto you… blessed are all they that wait for him.'

"We must wait, you see, and count our blessings." He stopped his measured pacing, planted his feet firmly in front of his listeners and reminded them of the great famine that struck Samaria while the country was under siege by the Syrians. "They were so hungry that they would pay fourscore pieces of silver for an ass's head and five pieces of silver for a handful of bird's dung to eat." He paused to let the horror of eating bird's feces sink into their imagination. "Remember the Israelites wandering in the desert for forty years after leaving Egypt? Did God take care of them?" It was a rhetorical question, but he was elated at the nodding heads and murmured "Yesses." Emboldened by the audience involvement, he posed another question. "And how did God rescue them?" The response was immediate. Like a chorus from an old Greek tragedy came an incantation of "manna from heaven," delivered with Southern Baptist pride.

He strode behind the pulpit, glanced at the Judge's watch and said, with an audible sigh, "My time is up. But we can all know that God's time is never up. He's always with us, loving us and blessing us when we don't deserve His mercy."

He suddenly realized that he was tired, limp. A trickle of sweat eased from his armpit. From the front row came the tremulous voice of toothless ninety-year-old Chambers Cox: "God is great."

It was the cue for the congregation to ritually end the service: "God is good."

Junior had the last word: "God is great; God is good, all the time." And he dismissed them with a passionate prayer, completely forgetting to offer the traditional invitation to join the church.

But the church treated him with such warmth at leave-taking that he felt as if he had had a transfusion of some kind of manna from heaven.

That buoyant feeling lasted for a few weeks, a time in which he basked in a glow created by a devoted flock who gradually accorded him the respect he had always been denied. He delivered infinite versions of his original message. Under the influence of Junior's spiritual guidance, church members ate their collards and fried fatback, their eggs and grits, without complaint, remembering that things could be worse — they could be eating asses' heads and bird's dung.

But a cruelly cold winter broke their spirits, and the optimism waned. People tried to buck up and take care of each other, but there was less and less evidence of God's greatness and goodness.

A story went around that Buddy Mack, the town's homeless black man, had been seen eating corn kernels from cow patties in Mr. Hasty's barnyard. Nobody believed it, but little Cal Adams slipped off from his parents and went in search of the demented old man. He found him frozen dead on the ground, his hand on the door handle of a ruined storm pit. The stiff body was shrouded in icicles hanging from his limbs and from the drooling of the underlip. The sight so unnerved the child that he was left with a permanent stutter.

Chambers Cox deserted his amen pew, trying to avoid pneumonia and the Grim Reaper. Widow Boyd, Chambers' stalwart Christian buddy, apologized to Junior for Chambers' absence, but she, too, succumbed to hardship and soon no longer ventured out. By mid-February, Junior had discontinued the Wednesday night prayer service for lack of attendance. He spent more time digging graves in ice-encrusted ground than in preparing sermons. Again and again, he stood at graveside, often shaking from driving rain and whipping cold wind, trying to give comfort with the ageless words "In my Father's house are many mansions: If it were not so, I would have told you. I go to prepare a place for you."

When he stood beside the clumsily built pine coffin holding little Sally Jane, tortured to death by whooping cough, he quoted Revelations, which promised that "there shall be no more death, neither sorrow, nor crying, neither shall there be any more pain." He did not try to analyze why he was more concerned about his wet feet than about the baby's soul. But he did have the grace to feel guilty about it later.

When the consumptive Baptist minister passed away, Junior tried to bury him with spiritual flair and delivered his "O, death, where is thy sting?" passage in an oration worthy of a Shakespearean actor playing King Lear. This time, when he did not feel guilty over his pretentious performance, he wondered if he might not be spiritually bankrupt.

The weeks stumbled by with unrelenting hardship, and Junior found it increasingly hard to justify the ways of God to man. When the Anse house burned to the ground from live embers in the fireplace ashes Josh Anse had thrown out, the old man hobbled on his club foot to the church steps, where his pastor found him. Clutching a dying yellow cat that smelled of burned flesh, he watched the orange flames lick at the sky and told Junior to take his prayers and go to hell.

The man of God didn't have much better luck with counseling the Barnet brothers, who knifed each other on a regular basis over the issue of who was to blame for the collapse of their sawmill. Junior visited them in jail and appealed to their finer instincts to work for family harmony. But they turned on him, ridiculing his suspect religious conversion and hurling outhouse language and obscene invective at his retreating back.

He felt more and more reluctant to emulate Isaiah's appeal to God to "Send me." And he began to have a strange obsessive feeling that there was malignant evil abroad in the universe. He saw that evil personified in Screamersville in the form of a dark hobo who jumped off a boxcar as the L & N train slowed for the town and then roared away.

The man was the epitome of the feared mysterious hobos who prowled through towns during the Depression, begging for food and shelter. Slouched into a ragged black overcoat, the man had the hard-bitten look of a prison inmate with his sooty-looking complexion and a scar that whitely slit his thick lips. Junior saw him one day huddled against the locked door of the forsaken hardware store. He would not have been surprised to see cloven hoofs on the man. So he was not surprised (horrified but not surprised) when the nameless menace crashed through the door of Miss Rosa Appleby's house, raped her viciously and forced her to watch him consume everything edible in the kitchen. When Junior visited her later, she was so pitiful that he was conscience-stricken when he had the insane urge to tease her about having been robbed of her greatest antique — her virginity. Not finding "rape" in the concordance of his Bible, he fumbled through some woefully inappropriate Scripture passages and hurried away in confusion and chagrin.

He seized on the idea that Screamersville was in such dire peril that he could not save it — not as a Renaissance man, a physician, or a preacher. Everywhere he looked, he saw Satan "going to and fro in the earth, and walking up and down in it." He thought that Job's archetypal tester was prancing in glee when he took his mother to see the damage at her late sister's deserted antebellum home. On the day of their visit, the weather seemed bizarre, with still clouds threatening something ominous. Junior remembered that in the Bible a cloud was often the sign of God's presence and protection. Well, he wasn't buying that symbolism in twentieth-century Alabama. The cloud was more likely the work of the devil, he thought.

Rosemount, with its grand hand-hewed Ionic columns, was still the state's best example of Greek Revival architecture and Screamersville's proud symbol of faded glory. The poor whites who had lived in the caretaker's cottage had stripped the mansion of its priceless furnishings and left the house open to the weather and animals. Reba Scoggins stood in the grand ballroom, looked up at the gaping hole where the magnificent chandelier had been, and cried bitterly. "It's a desecration," she lamented.

"Now, Mama," Junior chided. "It's not a temple."

"It is to me," she insisted, peeking into a small parlor. "Oh," she said, a little catch in her throat, "there's where Grandfather kept his Stradivarius." She pointed to a space where a glass display case had held the beloved violin.

But Junior was not tempted into her nostalgia. Preoccupied with the entrance into the magnificent drawing room of a gaunt Jersey cow, his imagination turned the lowing bovine into an image of Satan going to and fro and shitting contemptuously on the Carrera marble floor built with Southern pride.

At the sight of the defecating cow, Reba shrieked, but the sound was lost in a cracking and rolling of thunder that shook the ruined edifice.

"We'd better get out of here," Junior yelled at her, but the roaring out of the west was unmistakable. And in the instant in which Junior felt the presence of the old diabolical snake from the Garden of Eden, the tornado took them.

It dropped them a quarter mile away in a rock-filled gully, his mother hysterical, bruised and cut, and he with a broken leg and tormented by fear of both God and Satan.

He heaved a malevolent rock off his crushed leg and gazed in stupefied wonder at the nearby gaunt cow that had accompanied them on their tornadic journey. There she was, like a bovine cadaver, centered in a spotlight of butter yellow sunshine, chewing a low-calorie cud in slow motion. Just at the moment when the scene seemed to be the epitome of blessed pastoral serenity, the cow hoisted her tail and desecrated God's green earth with just as little regard as she had defaced the marble mansion floor. Junior was sure the cow was a symbol of something mythic, but he couldn't quite figure out what.

After a month of recuperation, he took his fishing pole and theological questions to the bank of Coon's Creek. Spring had slipped in overnight, drenching everything in an avalanche of green, and the sun was pleasantly warm on the back of his neck.

He forgot about his colossal spiritual ignorance as the bobbing line enticed him into the warm womb of fisherman's paradise. He examined every catch he hauled in, looking for a God-eyed catfish. Three hours and nine fish later, when no winking fish had summoned him, he came to the conclusion that a fish is a fish, Coon's Creek is not the Sea of

Galilee, and a depression is a demonic puzzle.

He knew what he had to do. He went to the church and propped on the pulpit a big sign which read: "It's all smoke and mirrors. I quit. Amen." It was signed, "Your pastor, the Renaissance man."

Walking away, he wondered whatever happened to old Melly what's-her-name.

~Biographical Notes~

CB Anderson's stories have been published in the *North American Review, Crazyhorse, Iowa Review, Pleiades, New Millennium Writings,* and various other print and online venues. "Mavak Tov" is part of a recently completed collection titled *River Talk*. Grants from the Barbara Deming Fund and the Hedgebrook Colony as well as scholarships/fellowships from Bread Loaf, Stonecoast and the Prague Summer Seminars have supported her work. She teaches writing at Boston University.

Charles M. Boyer graduated from Beloit College with a junior year abroad at Manchester College, Oxford, England, and has an M.A. in fiction writing from the University of New Hampshire. He teaches English and Humanities at Montserrat College of Art, and previously taught at the University of New Hampshire and Northeastern University. He has published poems and short stories in such places *Abraxas, Literal Latte, The Larcom Review, The Atlanta Review* and other literary magazines. He received a grant for writing from the Wisconsin Arts Board and a Fellowship from the New Hampshire State Council on the Arts. His chapbook of poetry, *The Mockingbird Puzzle*, was published by Finishing Line Press. He lives in Wellesley, Massachusetts, with his family.

Gregg Cusick has been writing stories since he was a kid, and over the years he has supported his writing habits by working in construction, as an English teacher, as a paralegal and furniture mover, a retail manager and more. He received a Master's in English-Creative Writing from North Carolina State University in 1990. He currently tutors literacy and bartends in Durham, NC.

Emily Fridlund's fiction has appeared in *Boston Review, New Orleans Review, Southwest Review, Sou'wester, Painted Bride Quarterly,* and *The Portland Review*, among other journals. She grew up in the Twin Cities and received her MFA in fiction from Washington University in Saint Louis. Currently, she is pursuing her PhD in Literature and Creative Writing at the University of Southern California. She is finishing her first novel, *History of Wolves*, and has recently moved with her husband to Ithaca, New York. "Catapult" was first published in *The Chariton Review*.

Tara Mantel won the ninth Tartt's First Fiction Award with her collection *Elemental*. Her stories have appeared in *Harpur Palate, The Gettysburg Review, Quarterly West, TriQuarterly, The Evansville Review*, and *The Southern Women's Review*. She is working on a new book.

Pat Mayer is the author of two novels, *Terminal Bend* and *The Cannibals Said Grace*. Her short fiction appears in the anthologies *Belles' Letters: Contemporary Fiction by Alabama Women, Climbing Mt. Cheaha: an Anthology of Stories by Emerging Alabama Writers*, and *A State of Laughter: Comic Fiction from Alabama,* and elsewhere. She has twice been nominated for the Pushcart Prize. She is also a writer of comic verse and was the 2007 winner of the Books-A-Million Book Sense World Limerick Competition. She lives in Mobile, Alabama with her husband, Paul.

Dan Pope's novel, *Housebreaking*, is forthcoming from Simon & Schuster in May 2014.

Born and raised in Abilene, Texas, **Mary Helen Specht** has a BA in English from Rice University and an MFA in creative writing from Emerson College, where she won the department's fiction award. Her writing has been nominated for multiple Pushcart Prizes and appeared in numerous publications, including: *The New York Times, The Colorado Review, Michigan Quarterly Review, The Southwest Review, Florida Review, Southwestern American Literature, World Literature Today, Blue Mesa, Hunger Mountain, Bookslut, The Texas Observer,* and *Night Train*, where she won the Richard Yates Short Story Award. A past Fulbright Scholar to Nigeria and Dobie-Paisano Writing Fellow, Specht teaches creative writing at St. Edward's University in Austin, Texas. She is at work on a novel.

After a brief stint as a newspaper reporter in Birmingham, **Betty Jean Tucker** has lived in the Alabama Black Belt town of Linden. She holds three degrees, including a Ph.D. from the University of Alabama. For twenty years she was a professor of English and chairperson of the Division of Languages and

Literature at Livingston University (now the University of West Alabama). "The Renaissance Man" is one of a collection of Depression era stories entitled, *On a Darkling Plain*, which will be published by Livingston Press in 2014. Betty Tucker grew up in that Great Depression.

Joe Taylor has directed Livingston Press at The University of West Alabama for over twenty years. He has four story collections published. A novel of his, *The Theoretics of Love,* is forthcoming from NewSouth Books. He has just completed *Pineapple*, a comic novel in rhyming quatrains (mostly).

Patricia Taylor has been a registered nurse for thirty-seven years and is presently working on a story collection of her experiences. She has been an editor for all the past Tartts contests. She has twelve dogs and three cats, who all have the run of the house.

www.ingramcontent.com/pod-product-compliance
Lightning Source LLC
Chambersburg PA
CBHW030518260626
47157CB00005B/1798